LOVE DOWN UNDER

What Reviewers Say About MJ Williamz's Work

"MJ Williamz, in her first romantic thriller has done an impressive job of building up the tension and suspense. Williamz has a firm grasp of keeping the reader guessing and quickly turning the pages to get to the bottom of the mystery. *Shots Fired* clearly shows the author's ability to spin an engaging tale."—*Lambda Literary*

"*Forbidden Passions* is 192 pages of bodice ripping antebellum erotica not so gently wrapped in the moistest, muskiest pantalets of lesbian horn dog high jinks ever written. Within the first few pages we're greeted with fluttering crotches, burning loins, and the swell of young breasts. But, the erotica connoisseur need not worry, the slow start is intentional, and the pace and heat picks up considerably from there."—*The Rainbow Reader*

Visit us at www.boldstrokesbooks.com

By the Author

Shots Fired

Forbidden Passions

Initiation by Desire

Speakeasy

Escapades

Sheltered Love

Summer Passion

Heartscapes

Love on Liberty

Love Down Under

LOVE DOWN UNDER

by

MJ Williamz

2017

ISBN 13: 978-1-62639-726-2

This Trade Paperback Original Is Published By
Bold Strokes Books, Inc.
P.O. Box 249
Valley Falls, NY 12185

First Edition: February 2017

Credits
Editor: Cindy Cresap
Production Design: Susan Ramundo
Cover Design By Sheri (graphicartist2020@hotmail.com)

Acknowledgments

As always, I'd like to thank Radclyffe and Sandy for giving my book a home. Thank you to all my Bold Strokes family for their support and encouragement. A special thanks to Cindy, my editor, for her constant work to make me a better author.

I would be remiss if I didn't thank Sarah for reading this book for me and helping me with her hands-on knowledge of Australia.

And, of course, a huge thank you to Laydin, whose undying love keeps me going.

Dedication

For Laydin—without whom none of this would be possible.

Chapter One

Wylie Boase stepped out of the airport into the warm Australian air. The breeze felt good on her face after her two days in airports and on planes. The fresh air felt good in her lungs. She pulled her backpack closer around her and glanced around for the minibus that would take her on her adventure. She saw the red and black circle of Dingo Tours on a bus, and with growing excitement, walked over.

A beautiful redhead was standing outside the bus, talking to others who had gathered around her.

"Is this where I'm supposed to be?" Wylie said.

"If you're on your way to Broome, this might be the place," the woman replied with a smile in her softly accented voice. She spun Wylie around and patted her backpack. "You look like you belong with us."

"My name's Wylie Boase."

The redhead looked over the list in her hand.

"Welcome, Wylie. I'm Sheila. I'll be your guide."

"Great. When do we get started?"

"You were the last one we were waiting for, so we can get going now."

Wylie stashed her backpack on the rack and took a seat. She watched the buildings and traffic disappear as they left Perth behind them. She listened to the melodic tone of Sheila's voice as they drove. Was it her imagination or did Sheila spend most of her time looking at her?

She relaxed for a while until they entered a national park and came to a beautiful desert. Later on, the bus stopped and they were allowed to sandboard down the massive dunes of Jurien Bay.

Wylie already felt freer. She was at one with nature out in the sand, in the heat. But no matter what she did, Wylie kept her eyes on Sheila. There was something about her that challenged her. She seemed flirtatious with limits. Wylie wanted to find out what those limits were and break through them. Sheila was a tall woman who stood only a few inches shorter than Wylie. She was slim of build, with pert breasts that bounced beautifully as the bus made its way from place to place.

Wylie made another run down the dunes before walking over to talk to Sheila.

"This must get old for you, huh?" she said.

"What? Seeing people enjoying themselves?" Sheila said. "Not a chance. I love my job."

"Really? That's great. Not many people I know can say that. Still, seeing the same things all the time can't be that fun."

"I love my country. I think it's beautiful. I love all it has to offer. So, yes, it is fun for me."

Wylie smiled.

"It's a beautiful country. At least what I've seen of it, and I've only been here a few hours."

"If you get tired of sandboarding, you should walk down to the beach," Sheila said.

"Come with me?"

"Sure." She smiled.

They walked along the soft sand, closer together than they needed to be, but Wylie wasn't complaining. As they got to the water, they saw seals bobbing there, begging for fish. Wylie wished she had something to throw the cute creatures, but she had nothing.

"We should get back to the others," Sheila said. "We have more to see today."

"Sounds good."

As they turned, Sheila lost her footing and fell into Wylie, who held her up. Sheila's arms went around her to balance herself. Wylie held her a little longer than was necessary. Sheila didn't seem to mind.

"Are you okay?" Wylie said.

"Yes. A little embarrassed. My foot just got caught in the sand. I'm fine now. Thank you."

"My pleasure."

Wylie watched as a light blush crept over Sheila's face. It only added to her beauty.

Everyone got back on the bus and they continued their journey, which led them through the port city of Geraldton and on to Horrocks where they would spend the night.

Wylie had already fallen in love with the Coral Coast of Australia. While she was excited about getting to Broome, she was certainly enjoying the ride to get there. When the bus stopped in Horrocks, she grabbed her backpack and stepped off the bus, looking around at her gorgeous surroundings. The grass was green, the palm trees swayed, and the air smelled of salt water. The dunes had shrubbery growing on them, but past that was beautiful turquoise water. She couldn't wait to get in.

The group filed into the hostel where they'd be spending the night. Clothes were quickly removed and swimsuits put on. Wylie wore her board shorts and a T-shirt. She made short order of changing so she could catch a glimpse of Sheila slipping into her suit. She wasn't disappointed. Sheila's body was long and lean, and Wylie knew she'd have to have her at some point. She didn't know how or when, but the reaction in her body was strong and she was sure Sheila was feeling it, too.

The spring evening was warm and Wylie longed to get in the water, but first, she followed the rest of her group out to the platform to see if they could catch a glimpse of any migratory humpback whales. It wasn't for naught, though, as they saw a pod swim by. Wylie was as excited as the rest of her companions.

They made their way back to the beach where Wylie quickly sought out Sheila.

"So these waters are safe to swim in? I've heard rumors of sharks and jellyfish here in Australia."

Sheila laughed.

"This is a protected beach. You've got nothing to fear swimming here."

"Are you getting in?" Wylie asked. She longed to see Sheila's long red hair cascading down her back and her wet swimsuit clinging to her figure.

"I'm thinking about it."

"I will if you will."

"I'm sure you will even if I don't," Sheila said.

Wylie grinned.

"Maybe," she said. "But I'd enjoy it more with you."

There. She'd said it. Now it was up to Sheila. Wylie felt a tug of nerves, but she quickly pushed them down. She wanted Sheila and was determined to confirm that Sheila was into her as well.

"Fine," Sheila finally said. "I'll go in with you."

They waded out into the water. The waves were small and manageable. When they got to their waists, Sheila dove in and surfaced just as Wylie had hoped. Head back and breasts pushed up, she was a sight for sore eyes.

"What?" Sheila said, and Wylie realized she was staring.

"Nothing. It's just…you're beautiful."

There was that blush again.

"And you, my dear Wylie, are a player."

"Perhaps I am."

"Well, turnabout's fair play. Let's see you dive in and come up and I'll tell you if I think you're beautiful."

Wylie had no comeback. She didn't consider herself beautiful by any standard. Handsome, maybe, but she didn't like to be called pretty or beautiful. She was too masculine for that. Still, a dare had been made and she wasn't about to back down.

She dove into the warm water and surfaced, nowhere near as elegantly as Sheila had. Instead of her hair brushing back, it fell onto her forehead and dripped water in her eyes. She pushed it back and smiled at Sheila.

"Well?"

"Very nice," Sheila said. "Though beautiful isn't the right word. You're definitely easy on the eyes. And you have a great body, by the way. What do you do for a living?"

"I'm a brick layer."

"Ah, manual labor. No wonder you're built that way. Let me see your hands."

Slightly embarrassed, Wylie held out her hands. Sheila took them and looked at her palms.

"You work hard. Your hands show it."

"They're not too rough, though," Wylie said. "I keep them as soft as I can."

"In deference to the ladies, no doubt."

"No doubt."

"Come on. Let's swim."

Wylie stood there as Sheila took off, slicing through the water like a pro. With no real option, she took off after her. Wylie was an accomplished swimmer herself and soon caught up with Sheila.

They swam out to the reef then turned around and swam back to shore, where they found a beach hut, basically an open roofed structure on the sand. They made themselves comfortable beneath it.

"That was refreshing," Sheila said.

"It was. It felt good to get out there and exercise after sitting in that bus most of the day."

"And your plane ride before that. You must be exhausted."

Wylie had forgotten about her flight. She had been too excited all day to worry about being tired. There was too much to see to worry about sleeping.

"I'll sleep when I'm dead," she said.

Sheila laughed.

"Somehow that attitude suits you."

"Why, thank you. I'd say you already know me pretty well."

"Smooth, Wylie. So you probably think I know you well enough to sleep with you."

"You said it. Not me."

"No, but you thought it," Sheila said.

"And?" Wylie arched an eyebrow.

"And?"

Wylie leaned forward and cupped Sheila's jaw. She lightly dragged her thumb along her cheek. Looking in her eyes, she saw a desire that matched her own. She lowered her mouth and brushed her lips. Sheila tasted of salt and fresh air. And Wylie wanted more.

She pulled away, though, determined to be sure this is what Sheila wanted. Wylie had no problem getting women, it was true, but she'd be damned if she'd pursue someone not interested.

"That was nice," Sheila said.

"Yes, it was."

"May I have another?"

"Of course."

Wylie moved closer to Sheila on the bench. She reached her hand behind Sheila's head and pulled her to her. She kissed her harder this time and ran her tongue along Sheila's lower lip. The kiss left her lightheaded. She was about to pull away again when Sheila opened her mouth and invited Wylie's tongue in.

She was more than happy to oblige. Sheila's mouth was warm and moist, and their tongues moved in a rhythm Wylie wanted their bodies to move to. She pulled Sheila closer until their bodies were pressed together. She could feel the rise and fall of Sheila's firm breasts against hers and was instantly wet.

She moved her hand down Sheila's back and brushed the side of her breast. She longed to run her fingers over her nipples, to take them in her mouth and suck them, but exercised self-control. It wasn't easy, but she managed. The night was dark and many of the others had already gone to bed. Still, there were a few stragglers.

Sheila grabbed her hand and moved it away.

"Not yet," she said.

"Sorry. I can't help myself."

"Come back to my room with me."

"Your room?"

"I have a private room. Usually, I stay with the campers, but tonight, I want you all to myself."

"Lead the way."

"I have my own room, but the showers are shared," Sheila explained. "So if you want to take a shower…"

"I do. Point the way."

Wylie padded down the hall to the shower and quickly stripped out of her sandy, salty swimwear. She stepped into the shower, hoping the water would do something to alleviate the need that had all but consumed her. It did not, but it still felt good to be clean. She wrapped a towel around her and went back to Sheila's room.

"All better?" Sheila said.

"All clean anyway. Only one thing is going to make me better."

"Patience, my dear American. Patience. I'm off to take my shower now."

"I'll be in bed."

"Oh, I look forward to that sight."

"Hurry back."

"I will."

But she didn't. It seemed like forever that Wylie lay in that small bed alone, yearning for a chance at Sheila's body.

Sheila finally returned, a towel wrapped around her body and one around her hair. The beauty of her naked face was not lost on Wylie. She rolled over onto her back and laced her fingers behind her head.

"What are you doing?" Sheila said.

"Watching you."

"Yeah?"

"Yeah. What took you so long?"

"I wasn't that long, loverboi. You're just in a hurry."

"I suppose I am. I'm itching to get at you. I admit that."

Sheila unwrapped her hair and bent over to shake it out. She flipped it back behind her and stood staring at Wylie. Only one thing stood between them. Wylie lost her patience. She climbed out of bed and crossed the room. She stood looking down at Sheila who had never taken her gaze off her.

"Your body is amazing," Sheila said.

"So is yours. Now, may I see it?" She stood with her hand on the towel, awaiting permission to remove it.

Sheila put her hands on Wylie's shoulders.

"You may do whatever you like."

"I do like the sound of that."

Wylie untucked the towel from its confines and held it as it fell open. Her breath caught at the perfectly formed body she was looking at. Sheila wasn't muscular like Wylie. Instead she was soft in all the right places.

"My God, you're amazing," she whispered.

Wylie kissed Sheila's forehead, her cheeks, and finally her mouth. She took her hand.

"Let's get in bed."

"There's not a lot of room," Sheila said.

"We'll make do."

She led Sheila to the bed and let her lay down. She lay down next to her, on her side, and propped herself up on an elbow.

"I could look at you for hours on end."

"I hope you don't plan on just looking," Sheila said.

"Oh, no. I have big plans for you."

Wylie moved her hand over the length of Sheila's body, from end to end, over and over again.

"Your skin is so soft," she said.

Sheila said nothing, only watched Wylie's hand on its mission.

Wylie brought her hand back up to finally skim her palm over a rock hard nipple.

"Your body is so responsive."

"You're making me crazy," Sheila said.

"Good."

Wylie took the nipple in her mouth while her hand massaged the firm breast. She flicked the tip of the nipple with her tongue and tugged it further in her mouth. Sheila grabbed her head and held it in place.

Wylie moved to the other nipple and did the same to it. By this time, Sheila was moving on the bed next to her, writhing her hips into the mattress.

"You like that?" Wylie looked into her eyes.

"Oh God, yes."

Wylie went back to suckling on the nipple while she pinched and tugged on the other. She wanted more, wanted to devour every inch of Sheila, but was determined to go slow. She wanted Sheila to have the time of her life. And she was just the woman to give it to her.

Sheila's breathing became labored and Wylie wondered if she could get her off with just nipple play. She was determined to find out. She kept it up, and soon Sheila cried out.

"You're easy," Wylie said.

"You're good."

Wylie just grinned and kissed down Sheila's belly. It was soft and smooth and tasted like soap. She continued kissing lower until she came to where Sheila's legs met. She kissed down one inner thigh and up the other. She nibbled and sucked as she went, careful not to leave any marks, though she would have loved to have branded Sheila as hers, at least for the next few days.

She finally moved her mouth to Sheila's center and lapped at the juices flowing there. She sucked her swollen lips before licking her hardened clit. She pulled it between her own lips and ran her tongue around it. She could feel it pulsing and knew Sheila was close.

Wylie dipped her fingers inside Sheila and stroked her satin walls. Two fingers, then three, she plunged deeper and deeper. Sheila rose to greet each thrust. She ran her tongue over the tip of Sheila's clit and that's all it took. Sheila cried out her name as she came again and again.

"Oh, my God," Sheila said when she finally caught her breath. "That was mind-blowing."

"I'm glad you enjoyed it." Wylie kissed her way back up Sheila's body and finally kissed her mouth. "You are a lot of fun."

"We'll see how much fun I am," Sheila said.

She rolled over so Wylie was on her back and she was over her. She kissed her hard on her mouth and slipped her tongue between Wylie's lips.

Wylie was a wet throbbing mess by this point and hoped Sheila didn't have plans to tease her too badly. She wasn't sure she wouldn't come at her first touch.

Sheila bent over Wylie's nipple and breathed hot air on her. The sensation was arousing as hell and Wylie almost cried at its effect. Sheila lowered her mouth and sucked the nipple deep into her mouth. Wylie arched off the bed at the feel of it. Her nipples were hardwired to her clit and her clit twitched with anticipation of what was to come.

Sheila didn't release her nipple, she continued to suck and lick it as she ran her hand down Wylie's body. She slid it between her legs and rubbed her clit, which was hard and ready. Wylie closed her eyes and bit her lip, pleading with herself not to come too soon. Sheila felt so good and Wylie needed this so badly.

She arched her back again, urging Sheila lower. Sheila seemed to understand as she slipped her fingers inside. Wylie moved her hips, greeting everything Sheila was giving her and adding to the pleasure. She reached between her legs and grabbed Sheila's hand and placed it on her clit. Together they rubbed, their hands sliding over each other in the slick juices, until Wylie moaned through clenched teeth, the orgasms tearing through her body.

They lay there in satiated silence for a few minutes.

"I suppose I should get back to the hostel, huh? It wouldn't be cool for them to find me here in the morning," Wylie said.

"I suppose that's true."

"Will we have a dorm room again tomorrow night?"

"Yes, we will."

"Most excellent."

Wylie slipped into her wet swim attire and snuck out into the night.

CHAPTER TWO

The following morning came very early to Wylie. She went with the others to the mess hall and gratefully chugged several cups of coffee, as well as enjoyed the breakfast they served. She had yet to see Sheila and hoped things wouldn't be too awkward between them. They were both adults and what they had done was natural. And it had been a hell of a good time.

She had just sat down with her fifth cup of coffee when she felt a hand brush her shoulders just as she heard Sheila's voice.

"Finish up, everyone. We have another big day ahead of us."

Wylie turned to face her.

"How are you today?"

"Great. And you?"

"Exhausted."

"You had a long day yesterday," Sheila said. "Maybe tonight you'll sleep better."

"What did I say before?"

"You'll sleep when you're dead."

"Exactly."

Wylie bussed her table and put her backpack on to walk to the bus. She felt like a loner in the group. Others had made friends already, but she had been so focused on Sheila, she hadn't really reached out to anyone else. No loss. She still had a few days before they reached Broome, at which point she'd never see any of them again. So if she made friends, great. If not, she'd be fine.

The day's trip was through beautiful country. They drove to Kalbarri National Park, where they explored the beautiful Murchison Gorge. Wylie thought she'd never seen a place so pristine. The red rock formations were stunning and the view of the river amazing.

She joined a group who hiked all the way down to the river and went for a swim. The cool dip was refreshing after the long hike in, and the view from the bottom of the gorge was equally as stunning, if not more so, than the view from the top.

Wylie got her camera out and took dozens of pictures of the area. She made a mental note to come back and explore the area again. She felt alive and exuberant as she hiked back up to where the rest of the group waited.

She sat next to Sheila as they ate their lunch.

"So, are you Aussie born and bred?" she asked.

"No. I was born in Ireland. We moved here when I was four."

"Ah. That explains the name."

"Yes. Sheila is a woman, not a name here."

"Well, it fits you," Wylie said. "Because you're all woman."

She was rewarded with another blush.

"You blush easily, do you know that?"

"You make me blush. That doesn't surprise me."

"It's cute."

"You know, anyone could hear us talking."

"No. We're sitting downwind and I'm being very quiet. Don't worry. I'd never compromise your honor."

"I appreciate that." Sheila laughed.

"What's so funny?"

"You are. You're so chivalrous and yet you were so bold hitting on me yesterday."

"I only hit on you because you wanted to be hit on."

"How would you have known that?" Sheila said.

"You were flirting with me all day."

"I was not."

"If you weren't, then how did I feel the need to hit on you and why did you accept and how did we end up in bed?"

Sheila laughed again.

"I honestly don't know. I'll admit I found you attractive the minute you walked up to me, but I can't believe I was that obvious."

"You were subtle, but I could read the signs."

"Well, I guess I'm glad you could."

"Me, too." Wylie smiled.

They climbed back in the bus and continued on their journey. Next stop was at Shell Beach. The white shelled beach made a striking contrast with the clear green water. The water called to Wylie, and she kept her swim shoes on as she made her way to it. Sheila had told them that the water had twice the salt content as regular beaches and Wylie was determined to experience swimming in it.

She couldn't get over the amount of shells on the beach. That's all there were, millions of shells, stretched along the coast. She crunched to the water and stepped in. She could immediately feel the difference between this and regular salt water. It was thick, heavy. She swam for a bit, then went back to the bus with her other travelers. They chattered together about their experience until Sheila told them they were on their way to their final destination of the day.

Wylie was fidgety. She was so excited to get to Shark's Bay and all it had to offer. She was particularly looking forward to Monkey Mia. Swimming with dolphins had long been one of her dreams. And it was about to come true. She knew they didn't have far to go, but she could barely stand the anticipation.

They arrived at Shark's Bay, and Sheila gathered them all outside the bus.

"There is plenty to do here. I want you all to enjoy yourselves. I'll be here if you have any questions. We'll meet back here to drive over to the hostel at six. Don't be late. They will have prepared dinner for us. Enjoy your day, everyone."

As people dispersed, Wylie stood back and waited to talk to Sheila.

"Really?" she said. "You don't get to come see the sights with us?"

"Really. I have to stay here with the bus. Now go. See what you want to see while you have time. Be back here by six."

"I will. I'll see you then."

Wylie followed the signs to the dolphins and was soon swimming with them. The bottlenoses swam right up to her and let her stroke them. It felt like she was petting rubber, only there was more to it than that. And the dolphins seemed to love her. There were others waiting their turn, so she had to finally give up her spot. But she knew the experience would last a lifetime.

Next on order was a snorkeling adventure. She joined a group on its way to Surf Point, an area with good coral cover and an abundance of fish in shallow water. She loved the water and had a blast watching the colorful fish swim around. She'd contemplated SCUBA diving, but thought, since she had such limited time, that snorkeling would be a better idea. And she was happy she had.

She got back to the bus right at six, and she was happy to see she wasn't the last one.

"How was your afternoon?" Sheila asked her.

"It was amazing."

"Did you swim with the dolphins?"

"I did. And I snorkeled around Surf Point."

"I've done that. It's beautiful."

At last, the stragglers joined them and they drove off to the hostel.

Dinner was served, and Wylie made a point of sitting next to Sheila.

"So, tell me how you ended up with this job," she said.

"I took the job while I was at university. It was on holidays only so it worked out with my schedule. Then I found I loved it. The pay's not bad when you work full-time. And as I said yesterday, I love my country. I think it's beautiful and I love sharing that with others."

"You do a great job. I mean that. You're a wonderful guide. And you really know your stuff and it shows."

"Why thank you."

"You don't need to blush at a compliment."

"Apparently, I do." She laughed.

"You're too cute," Wylie said.

The blush deepened.

"You need to stop or I'll have to go sit somewhere else."

"No!" Wylie said. "Please don't. Please stay here with me. I'll behave. I promise."

"Okay." Sheila smiled.

Wylie sat back and again pondered her afternoon.

"What are you thinking about?" Sheila said.

"Just reliving my afternoon. I still can't believe it. I swam with dolphins, Sheila. I know to you that's not a big deal, but to me, it's a once in a lifetime experience."

"Oh, no, Wylie. Don't say it's not a big deal. It's a very big deal. I've only done it a few times myself. I know the sense of awe it creates."

"They're so intelligent and friendly."

"And trusting."

"Yes. Trusting. I suppose that's what truly separates them from humans, huh?"

Sheila arched an eyebrow at Wylie.

"Ah, so my new friend is a cynic, eh?"

"Not a cynic, really. Though, I suppose that did sound cynical, didn't it? Think about it, though. Humans don't trust each other. They can't, really."

"So, if I said I trust you, what then? Am I non-human? Or just a fool?"

"No, no, no. Individually we can trust each other, but as a species we can't."

"I don't understand," Sheila said.

"I mean generally speaking, we don't trust each other. That's why we have the troubles in the world that we do. But on an individual level, we can believe in each other. Does that make sense, now?"

"I suppose."

Wylie laughed.

"What's so funny?" Sheila said.

"All this because I swam with dolphins today. Who knew we'd have such a philosophical conversation."

"A good brain is as sexy as a nice body."

"I agree."

"I like how smart you are," Sheila said.

"And I, you."

"How did someone as smart as you end up working manual labor?"

"Just lucky, I guess."

"I don't know if that's an answer, but I suppose I'll take it."

Dinner was over then and people had started bussing their tables. There was a campfire burning, and they all made their way to it.

"May I sit next to you?" Wylie asked.

"I was hoping you would. Just behave."

"I'll do my best." Wylie laughed.

They all sat around the campfire, recounting their stories of the day. Everyone was in agreement that they had seen and done some wonderful things that day. Sheila answered questions and Wylie sat back and marveled at her knowledge. She was more attracted to her every moment and couldn't wait until bedtime when she would have her to herself.

Finally, the fire burned low and people wandered off, pleading exhaustion.

"How are you doing?" Sheila asked Wylie.

"I'm great. You ready for bed?"

Sheila blushed.

"I am."

"Let's go, then."

They walked down a sandy path to get to the dorms. Truth be told, she longed to sleep with Sheila, to hold her all night long and make love to her upon waking. She knew that wasn't going to happen. And she was thankful for what she got. When she'd made reservations for her trip, she'd expected to see Western Australia and eventually the Broome area. She'd never planned on meeting a wonderfully beautiful lover to pass her nights with.

They reached the dorm and each took her shower, just as they'd done the night before. When Sheila walked into the room, Wylie caught her breath. She couldn't believe how beautiful she was. Her skin radiated health and vitality. And the flush indicated desire.

Wylie patted the bed next to her and Sheila crossed the room to join her. She lay next to Wylie and propped herself up on an elbow.

"Tell me about yourself, Wylie Boase."

Wylie pulled her on top of herself and kissed her.

"What do you want to know?"

"Did you graduate from high school?"

"Is that important?" Wylie kissed down Sheila's neck.

"I'm just curious."

"I'll have you know I have a degree in business management."

"A degree? Why do you work manual labor?"

Wylie pulled back and looked at Sheila.

"Why is that such an issue for you?"

Sheila leaned in and kissed her.

"It's not an issue. It's just curious. I mean, shouldn't you be working in an office or some such?"

"Can you see me in an office?"

"Not really," Sheila said. "So, tell me why you're not using your degree."

Wylie brushed Sheila's hair back from her shoulder and kissed her there.

"I could have. But I didn't want to live in a city. I like the small college town where I went to school. So I stayed there and kept my job as a brick layer."

She kissed lower on Sheila until she kissed the top of her breast.

"Any other questions?"

"Um…no. Not right now."

"Good."

She kissed her hard on the mouth. It was a kiss that conveyed all the passion she was feeling.

"God, I want you," she murmured against Sheila's lips.

"Mm-hm."

She slipped her tongue in Sheila's mouth as she pressed their bodies together. The feel of their breasts pressed together caused moisture to pool between her legs. She opened her legs and Sheila pressed her thigh against her center.

"You're wet," Sheila said.

"Imagine that."

Wylie lay back and looked longingly at Sheila's body above her. She kneaded her breasts and pinched her nipples. Sheila bent over again and kissed her. Wylie wrapped her arms around her and pulled her close, while she wrapped her legs around Sheila's thigh. She moved up and down on it and reveled in the feel of Sheila's soft skin pressing against her hard clit. She was close, so very close. Her world tipped slightly off center. She pulled back. She stopped rubbing. Tempting though it was to let herself go, she was a firm believer in lady's first.

"Why'd you stop?" Sheila said.

"You first."

"Why?"

"It's just how I am."

Sheila sat up straight on Wylie. She played with her own breasts and tweaked her own nipples. Wylie's crotch spasmed. She was about to come again and she was determined not to.

"What are you doing?" she asked.

"Playing."

"You're going to make me come," Wylie croaked.

"I'm going to make me come."

"Oh, shit. Shouldn't I be helping?"

"Sure. You play with my tits."

"Gladly."

Wylie fondled and sucked her breasts and nipples until she heard Sheila moaning. The moaning was getting louder, so Wylie lay back on the bed and watched as Sheila pleased herself.

She was sitting back on Wylie's legs by then. Her legs were spread, and Wylie could see her hot pink pussy and swollen clit. She watched with rapt attention as Sheila rubbed faster and faster. Wylie put her hand over Sheila's and together they took her to an orgasm that had her shaking from head to toe.

Sheila fell backward onto Wylie's legs, which left her exposed to Wylie's admiring eyes.

"You are sexy as hell," Wylie said. She ran her hand over Sheila. "Sexy as hell."

"And now it's your turn," Sheila said.

She sat up and lay along the length of Wylie. Once again, she brought her knee between her legs.

"Oh, my. Now you're even wetter."

"Imagine that."

Wylie ground into Sheila's leg and Sheila pushed back against her.

"Oh, God, you feel good," Wylie said.

"So do you."

Sheila bent and took a nipple in her mouth. She tugged it deep inside her mouth and ran her tongue over it. She ran her hand down Wylie's body until she found her wet center. Using her knee for leverage, she thrust deep inside her. Over and over, she plunged inside while Wylie arched her hips to take each one.

The feeling was amazing. All focus was gone for Wylie save what was happening between her legs. She felt herself getting close and she arched higher, urging Sheila to thrust harder. Sheila did so. She thrust into Wylie one last time and Wylie shuddered, her whole body convulsed as she came.

CHAPTER THREE

Wylie held Sheila until she started to doze.

"Hey, you." Sheila nudged her. "You'd better get going."

"Mm. Do I have to?" Wylie snuggled deeper against Sheila.

"Yes. You have to."

Wylie sat up.

"I know this. I just really don't want to."

"I don't particularly want you to. But it's how it has to be."

"Yeah." Wylie got up and dressed. She kissed Sheila and let herself out of her room and down to the common area.

She slept hard for the rest of the night, satiated from their lovemaking. And when Sheila came in to wake them the following morning, her hormones flared anew at the sight of her. She wanted to take her back to her room right then and ravish her. Instead, she stretched inside her sleeping bag, then climbed out to face the day.

The morning was spent with more time at Shark's Bay. Wylie was back at the dolphins first thing after breakfast. She spent several minutes simply taking pictures of the beautiful creatures and watching them frolic and play. Then, when she couldn't stand it any longer, she swam with them. She held their fins or simply swam next to them. She soaked up every minute of her allotted time and committed it to memory.

She still had some time to spend, so she snorkeled around Surf Bay again. Australia definitely agreed with her. She was glad she had decided to visit for vacation. She checked her watch and saw it was time to meet the others. She got out of the water, dried off, and headed to the bus.

Sheila was standing with a small group when she walked up. She turned.

"And here's Wylie," she said. "How was your morning?"

"Same as my afternoon yesterday. I love this place. I could spend all day with those dolphins."

"They are quite fun to swim with. That's for sure," Sheila said.

Other members of their group meandered toward them until they were all there. It was time to continue their journey. They stopped for lunch at a small coastal town where Wylie joined a group who were climbing rocks to see the view of the beach afforded there. It was breathtaking with steep rock walls surrounding them and the blue ocean far below them. They ate lunch then climbed back down for the last leg of the day's trip.

Late that evening, they arrived at Coral Bay. Wylie had heard stories of its beauty and longed to see it firsthand, but it was too dark when they arrived. That was fine with her. She would explore the following day. The fact that it was so late, meant that she had little time before she would get to climb into bed with Sheila again.

Dinner was served and she sat with Sheila.

"What will you be doing tomorrow?" Wylie asked.

"I don't know. This place is so beautiful. I never know what to do, you know, how best to enjoy its beauty."

"Is it really as spectacular as they say?"

"Look around you. Even in the dark, you can see how wonderful it is. Tomorrow you'll see how clear the water is. It's simply amazing."

"Would you like to snorkel with me?" Wylie said.

Sheila sat silently for a moment.

"What? Have you had other options?" Wylie said.

"No. It's not that. Wylie, you do know that this tour will end in a few days, right?"

"Sure I know that."

"And then we'll never see each other again."

"Right. Which is why I'd like to spend as much time with you now as I can," Wylie said.

"Okay," Sheila said. "As long as you know that."

The light clicked on in Wylie's head.

"You think I want a relationship?"

Sheila reached out and placed her hand on Wylie's leg.

"I didn't know. I just wanted us to be clear and open with each other."

"Oh, babe. You're sweet and smart and smokin' hot. Don't get me wrong. But I'm not looking for a relationship. I'm happy with just some fun."

"Oh good. That is such a relief."

"So, tomorrow? Snorkeling?"

"Sure thing," Sheila said.

"And tonight?" Wylie asked.

"Definitely." Sheila smiled.

"And when can we get started?"

"The others are starting to settle down. We should be able to make our way to my room soon."

They sat back and watched the moon play over the water. Wylie loved the different colors of the water. It was black in some places, yet green in others where the moonlight hit. She couldn't wait to get in that water tomorrow.

She was lost in thought when she felt the brush of Sheila's hand.

"Come on. Let's go to bed."

Wylie was up in a heartbeat. She took Sheila's hand and walked with her to her room.

They lay together in bed, enjoying the nearness of each other. Wylie kissed Sheila softly. She barely skimmed her lips.

"You're teasing me," Sheila said.

"Not really."

"Yes, really. Now come here and really kiss me."

Sheila pulled Wylie to her and held her there while she kissed her hard on her mouth. She opened hers and welcomed Wylie's tongue inside. They kissed like that for a few moments then Sheila pulled away.

"See? That was a kiss."

"I see," Wylie said. She rolled over on top of Sheila and kissed her again. She was lost in the feel of their tongues dancing together. She grew dizzy with passion and need, so she slid off her and kissed lower until she could close her mouth over one of Sheila's breasts.

Sheila moaned her appreciation and Wylie kept sucking while she moved her hand between Sheila's legs. She found her wet and ready for her. She never stopped suckling Sheila as she skimmed her fingers over her clit until she found her swollen lips. She tugged on them and rubbed them before slipping inside.

Sheila arched her hips to take Wylie deep. Wylie plunged as deep as she could go and ran her fingers along Sheila's walls. She thrust harder and harder and finally felt Sheila close tightly around her just as she cried out.

Wylie moved up to hold Sheila, but Sheila was in no mood to be held. She quickly moved down Wylie's body until she was between her legs. She nuzzled against her clit before lapping at her center. She slid her tongue in as deep as she could and licked up all the juices that were flowing there.

Sheila went back to Wylie's clit and sucked on it and ran her tongue over it. Wylie placed her hand on the back of Sheila's head. She didn't want her to move. She was close to an orgasm and didn't want Sheila to do anything to change that.

Sheila continued playing with Wylie's clit until Wylie arched off the bed and groaned loudly as she reached a powerful climax.

"Damn, woman," she said. "You sure know what you're doing."

"You're not so bad yourself."

"Get up here and let me hold you."

"No falling asleep," Sheila said.

"No. I won't." Wylie laughed, then asked, "What did you go to school for?"

"That's an odd post-coital question."

"Sorry. I've just been meaning to ask you."

"I wanted to be an architect."

"That's a far cry from tour guide," Wylie said. "I could understand marine biologist or something like that, but architect?"

"It's what I'd wanted to do since I was a little girl," Sheila said.

"Fair enough."

"Any other probing you need to do?"

"Well, now that you mention it…" Wylie rolled Sheila over and took her again, pleased with herself when Sheila called her name.

"That was wonderful," Sheila said.

"It was fun. But I should get going."

"Yes. I suppose you should. I wish you didn't have to."

"So do I, but that wouldn't look good on you, so I don't mind. I'll see you in the morning."

She kissed Sheila and made her way back to the women's area.

Wylie was up before the rest of the group the following morning. Excited about all the day held, she made her way to the dining area and helped herself to a cup of coffee. She took it outside and sat at a table and watched the sun come up.

The area went from darkness to beauty in a matter of minutes. Soon, the sun shone over the whole area, illuminating it all for her to take in. It was truly breathtaking with its white sandy beaches and clear water. She could even make out the reef from where she was sitting. She couldn't wait to get in the water and explore.

"You're up early," Sheila said from behind her.

"I am. Just watched the sunrise. It was spectacular."

Others had started coming out to enjoy the view so Wylie was careful to keep things as neutral as she could.

"How did you sleep?" she asked.

"Like a baby. You?"

"Same."

"Good. You ready for the day?"

"I was born ready."

"I don't doubt that." Sheila laughed. "Let's get some breakfast so we can get in the water."

They joined several others in line for food. Wylie had granola and fruit, determined not to fill up before snorkeling. They sat at a table with six other people.

"Is everyone having fun?" Sheila said.

Everyone said they were and they launched into a long discussion as to what had been their favorite activity so far. Hands down, swimming with the dolphins won out.

"What are you doing today?" Sheila asked them.

Some were going on the glass bottom boat, some were riding quads, and others, like them, planned to snorkel around the reef.

Everyone was in a great mood as dishes were cleaned, but Wylie knew no one was as excited as she was because she got to spend the day with Sheila. They quickly donned their swimsuits and made their way to the shore.

Wylie was excited to see the marine life of the area, but she was excited in a different way at the sight, once again, of Sheila in her suit. It clung to her body and showed off her figure. Wylie's palms itched to stroke her firm breasts and have her way with her.

"You look amazing," she whispered as she walked past her.

Wylie was already in the water up to her waist when Sheila joined her.

"You think you can just say something like that and walk on by?" she said.

"I think I did."

"Well, I think maybe you'll pay for it later."

"Now, doesn't that sound interesting?" Wylie said.

They set out to explore the reef and the varieties of fish that called it home. They were all shapes and sizes and came in dozens of colors. Wylie was impressed with the beauty of it all. They swam as long as they could and when they finally tired, they swam back to shore to relax.

"That was incredible," Wylie said. "I'm blown away at everything we saw."

She was breathing heavily, but didn't mind. They'd been swimming for quite a while with no break.

"I'm glad you enjoyed it. I can't take personal credit for its beauty, but I can take credit that it's in my country."

"Yes, you can," Wylie laughed.

"So, what now?" Sheila said.

"I want to take the glass bottom cruise."

"Really? Why? You've seen everything."

"Yes, but I'm guessin' the cruise will tell me what all I saw. You know, what fish was what and stuff. Come on. Have you ever taken it?"

"What? The cruise? No."

"Fine. We'll catch the next one out."

They caught the next cruise and relaxed and listened to their tour guide. Wylie drank some of the complimentary beer, while Sheila stuck with soda, saying it wouldn't do for her to be drunk on their bus tour.

The cruise was relaxing and informative, and when it ended, it was late afternoon and people started gathering around the bus.

"Go ahead and load up," Sheila said.

They did just that. When everyone was seated, they started on the next step of their adventure. Two hours later, they pulled in to Exmouth, where they'd be spending the night.

Wylie took in the sandy area that surrounded the small town and the red dirt that seemed to be prevalent in that area of the world. She turned her attention to the ocean side of the road and saw more white sandy beaches and clear water. She couldn't wait to get off the bus and into the water. The farther north they traveled, the more in love with Western Australia she became.

Dinner was simple, as usual, and after, Wylie followed Sheila to her room.

"I'm going to miss you when this tour is over," Sheila said.

"We have had some fun, haven't we?"

"And we still will. We have a few days left."

"Yeah. We're only halfway to Broome now, aren't we?" Wylie asked.

"That's about right."

They stood in the center of the room with Wylie's hands on Sheila's waist. She bent her head to taste Sheila's lips.

"I'm glad we still have some time," she said.

"Me, too. I'll definitely remember this particular tour fondly."

"Yeah. I will, too."

Wylie kissed her again, this time harder, more fiercely. She felt Sheila's arms go around her neck and pull her close. She tightened her own grip, relishing in the feel of Sheila's naked skin against hers. She felt her nipples poking in to her and had to pace herself, lest the moment be over too soon.

She walked Sheila over to the bed and Sheila sat. She dragged her hands all over Wylie's body.

"Your body never ceases to amaze me," she said. "You're so muscular and well-defined."

"Careful. You're playing with fire there."

"Yeah? You like the way I touch you?"

"I do."

Wylie struggled to stay upright as Sheila continued to touch her. She finally gently pushed Sheila back until she was lying on the bed. She dropped to her knees and placed Sheila's legs over her shoulders. She breathed in her scent as she spread her lips with her fingers.

She licked Sheila's clit as she buried her fingers inside her. She stroked all she felt in there as she sucked and lapped at her clit. In no time, Sheila had Wylie's head pressed against her. She raised her hips off her bed and clamped hard on Wylie's fingers as she reached her climax.

"Come here," Sheila said. "Lie with me."

Wylie climbed up on the bed and did as she was requested. She loved the feel of Sheila in her arms, so was happy to hold her. Her breath caught when she felt Sheila's hand between her legs. She rolled over on her back and spread her legs wide for her.

"I love how wet you get," Sheila said.

"How could I help it? You turn me on in a big way."

"Thank you. That's so nice to hear."

"Well, it's true. As you can tell."

"I can tell," Sheila said. She ran her fingers over the length of Wylie before delving deep inside. She played there briefly before moving her attention to Wylie's swollen clit. Wylie thought she'd split in half when she felt Sheila's light touch on it. She was so close already. She knew it wouldn't take much and the soft, gentle touch of Sheila's was almost too much to bear. Sheila finally rubbed her clit. She pressed into it as she rubbed it in circles, and soon it was Wylie's turn to cry out as she came again and again.

CHAPTER FOUR

Wylie awoke with the promise of a new day ahead. As well as the promise of another night with Sheila. There was something different about her. And if circumstances weren't as they were, she could see herself dating her seriously. But that wasn't to be, so she just accepted the fun they were having and smiled.

She climbed out of her sleeping bag as her hostel mates were doing the same. They wandered outside to find their breakfast waiting for them. As they ate, Sheila appeared and spoke to them.

"Today is your day to explore this beautiful area," Sheila said. "We don't offer any tours or anything like that. You're completely on your own. Of course, right now, I'm here to answer any questions, but then I'll be out exploring as well."

A few people had questions, but Wylie paid them no mind as she finished her breakfast. She was ready to hike along Yardie Creek. Then, she planned to swim in Turquoise Bay. She hadn't asked Sheila yet, but she was hoping she would join her.

Sheila finished answering questions and sat with Wylie.

"How are you this morning?" she asked.

"Great. And you?"

"I'm wonderful. This is one of my favorite days on the tour. What are you planning to do?"

"I plan to hike along Yardie Creek. I've heard it's beautiful."

"You haven't heard wrong. That sounds like a great way to spend the day."

"At least the first part of the day," Wylie said. "Then I want to play in Turquoise Bay, maybe even check out the lighthouse."

"Sounds great."

"What will you be doing?" Wylie asked.

Sheila sat quietly for a moment. She seemed to be thinking hard about something.

"Well," she finally said. "I was hoping to spend the day with you."

"I'd love that." Wylie smiled. "I was hoping you'd want to."

"Good. Then it's settled."

"Yes, it is. Oh. One more thing. Our tour doesn't include dinner tonight. I was wondering if you'd like to join me. I'm sure we can find a little spot in town."

"That would be great."

"Excellent."

People started dispersing from the hostel, and Sheila and Wylie joined the group heading up the gorge.

"The walls here are stunning," Wylie said.

"Yep. They never fail to impress me."

"I like the different colors."

"All due to erosion over the years."

"It's amazing what Mother Nature can do," Wylie said.

"Isn't it?"

They walked along, occasionally seeing some wildlife scurrying across the landscape.

After an hour and a half, they turned around and headed back. Some of the group kept going, some came with them.

"I wish I could hold your hand," Wylie said.

"So do I, but that wouldn't be very smart."

"No. I suppose not."

They got back to the hostel and changed into their swimsuits and grabbed their snorkeling equipment.

"We have a couple of options here," Sheila said.

"What might those be?"

"We can snorkel over there by the point, or we can drift snorkel down past the sand bar. Which would you prefer?"

"I'd love to drift snorkel. I love it when the small waves lull me along. I assume you're a strong enough swimmer to do that, too?"

"Of course I am," Sheila said.

"Great. Let's do that."

They walked out into the water and let the current guide them over the coral. They saw turtles and starfish and numerous colorful fish swimming by. Wylie thought it was some of the best snorkeling she'd ever done.

When they'd had enough, they swam back to shore and lay on the beach.

"That was incredible," Wylie said. "I can't believe all the species of fish we saw out there."

"There were many. That's true. And the colors. So vibrant."

"Yeah. That was one for the books."

"Indeed it was."

"Do you snorkel here every tour?"

"Most. I can't get enough of it."

"I don't blame you. I'd do it every day if I could."

"Too bad there's not a way to make a living out here," Sheila said. "It would be a great place to live."

"True. I suppose there's fishing, but I'm sure that's pretty competitive already."

They laid there until they were dry.

"I'm getting hungry," Wylie said.

"Me, too. Shall we go get changed for dinner?"

"We should."

They walked slowly back to the hostel and each headed for the shower. Wylie wished she could walk into the stall Sheila was using and properly sponge her up, but she knew better. Sheila could lose her job for her relationship with Wylie. So she behaved, hard though it was.

Wylie put on a pair of khaki cargo shorts and a blue golf shirt. It was the nicest outfit she'd brought with her. Sheila met her in front of the hostel in a long, flowered dress that clung to her top half, then billowed from the waist down. Wylie thought she'd never seen a more beautiful woman.

"Wow," she said.

"Wow, yourself. That shirt really brings out your blue eyes. You're more seductive than ever right now. I want to run my fingers through your short hair and pull you to me. I want to kiss you like you've never been kissed before."

"Sh. What if someone hears you?"

"There's no one around," Sheila said.

They strolled along the beachfront and found a restaurant right on the water. As soon as they were seated, Wylie ordered a beer and Sheila ordered a glass of wine.

"I wasn't sure you'd be allowed to drink," Wylie said.

"As long as I don't get snockered, it's okay."

"Well, good. I'm guessing you won't get drunk. I'd hate to take advantage of you."

"You needn't worry about that," Sheila said.

"Good."

They ordered their dinners and simply relaxed in each other's company.

"You're getting really dark," Sheila said. "The sun looks good on you."

"And you're getting more freckles," Wylie teased her.

"Story of my life. It's why I own stock in sunscreen companies. So I keep the freckles and don't get burned."

"That would be a drag, I'd think."

"It is what it is. It's how it's always been for me. I've gotten burnt a couple of times. Enough to know I never want it to happen again."

"I bet. You're so fair. I'd imagine it wouldn't take any time at all to fry."

"Exactly. So, I've never asked you. Where are you from? I know the US, but I don't know where," Sheila said.

"I'm from a small town in Northern California. I guarantee you've never heard of it. It's a college town. I went to school there and stayed. And you?"

"I'm from Sydney, I guess. We moved around a lot when I was little. But that's where my life in Australia started."

"Fair enough."

Their dinner arrived and they ate in a comfortable silence, with short conversations dotting the silence.

After, they went for a walk on the beach.

"How long are you in Australia?" Sheila asked.

"I don't know. I only have so much money budgeted. Maybe another week or two once we get to Broome."

"Oh, good. At least you'll have some time to bum around the area. It's a very beautiful part of our country."

"That's what I've heard. I can't wait to check it out."

The breeze off the water was warm and it brushed over Wylie like a lover's caress. Like Sheila's caress.

"We should get back to the hostel," she said.

"What's your hurry?"

"I want you."

"Is that right?"

"That's right. I want you and if you don't want me to lay you down right here, then we'd better head back to the hostel."

Sheila laughed. Music to Wylie's ears.

"Fine. Let's head back."

They hurried back to the hostel and went directly to Sheila's room. Sheila closed the door and was immediately in Wylie's arms.

"Do you have any idea what you do to me?" Wylie asked.

"I think I have a pretty good idea. You know, the knife cuts both ways."

"I'm happy to hear that."

Sheila pressed her body to Wylie's.

"So, you wanted to get back here. What are you going to do now?"

Wylie brushed a strand of Sheila's hair behind her ear.

"I'm going to have my way with you," Wylie said. She leaned in and nibbled Sheila's earlobe.

"I do like the sound of that." Sheila held fast to Wylie's shoulders.

Wylie kissed down her neck and kissed the bodice of her dress. She reached around behind her and deftly unzipped her dress. She helped Sheila step out of it, pleased to see she wore no undergarments. She stood naked for Wylie and Wylie grew wet admiring her form.

"You're beautiful," she said.

"You know it embarrasses me when you say that."

"But it's true. You are flat-out gorgeous."

"Thank you."

Sheila's body was a fine shade of pink thanks to Wylie's compliments, which only added to her attractiveness.

"You're so cute when you blush," Wylie said as she stripped off her own clothes. They lay together on the bed.

"I'm glad you think so since it's all I seem to do around you."

"I love your blushes."

"I hate them but can't do anything about them."

"I like the slight pink of your blushes as well as the bright red that covers your skin when you're flushed. You know, like when we've just finished making love."

Sheila's blush deepened.

"You're gorgeous," Wylie said before she bent to kiss her. She kissed her hard on her mouth and slid her tongue along Sheila's lower lip. Sheila tasted of sunshine and wine, and it made Wylie dizzy.

Sheila opened her mouth and Wylie slid her tongue inside. Their tongues danced together while Wylie ran her hand down Sheila's body. She smoothed it over one soft inner thigh then the other. She finally brought it to rest between Sheila's legs. She teased her clit as she rubbed circles around it without touching it. She moved her fingers lower and played with Sheila's lips.

Sheila spread her legs wider.

"Please. I need you."

"You do, huh?"

"Yes. Please, Wylie."

Wylie entered her then and felt her tightness surround her. She moved her thumb to Sheila's clit and Sheila cried out.

"That was fast," Wylie said.

"I was ready for you."

"You were? Since when?"

"Since breakfast." Sheila laughed.

"Fair enough," Wylie said.

"You're a very sexy woman," Sheila said. "With your short thick hair and those bedroom eyes. And a body that's hotter than hot. How could I not want you?"

"And this body is yours for the next several days."

"I know," Sheila said. "This makes me very happy. It makes it hard to concentrate on the bus when I'm supposed to be showing off the sights, but it makes me happy at night."

"Well, I'm kind of crazy about your body, too, you know. I love how responsive it is. And I love how you have curves in just the right places."

"I love how you love my curves." Sheila smiled as she played with Wylie's chest. "I'm so glad you're not a stone butch."

Wylie propped herself up on an elbow.

"Where did that come from?"

"I've just had stone butch lovers and I didn't enjoy them. I like to give as well as to receive and you let me."

"Hell yeah, I let you," Wylie said. "I'm so horny around you I can't see straight. I'd be a fool not to get some relief."

"Well, would you like some relief right now?"

"Now would be wonderful."

"Yeah?" Sheila nipped at Wylie's lip.

"Yeah." Wylie was throbbing. She was afraid she'd come before Sheila even touched her.

Sheila kissed down Wylie's neck to the little indentation of her shoulder. She nibbled down her chest and paused briefly to suck one nipple then the other. She licked down her stomach until she ended up between her legs.

She swirled her tongue around Wylie's clit and Wylie arched her hips off the bed. She felt her muscles clenching in their need. She moved her hips in rhythm with Sheila's tongue and in no time, her muscles released as wave after wave of orgasm washed over her.

"Wow," she said. "That was something else."

"You're something else. It's really a shame you can't stay the night."

"I know. Think of how much fun it would be to start our day that way."

"It would be wonderful. Unfortunately, it could also cost me my job."

"Fair enough," Wylie said. "I understand that."

She got out of bed and dressed. She kissed Sheila lightly on the lips.

"I'll see you tomorrow. Oh. One other thing. Would you like to catch a light breakfast with me tomorrow?"

"Oh yeah. I forgot. Breakfast isn't included tomorrow. That would be lovely."

"Great."

"Good night, Wylie."

"Good night."

Wylie woke before the others the next morning and crept down the hall to Sheila's room. She knocked lightly. There was no answer, so she knocked harder.

"Who is it?" Sheila said.

"It's me. Wylie."

Sheila opened the door and stood before Wylie dressed in a sheer nightgown that fell to the floor.

"You're gorgeous," Wylie said.

"And you're crazy. Why are you here?"

"I wanted to see if you were ready for breakfast."

"Ah, yes. Give me a moment to get ready."

Wylie pulled her close.

"We might have time for a little fun before we get breakfast."

Sheila playfully slapped Wylie's shoulder.

"I think not. If I'm going to lead the tour today, I need to have strength. I need a proper breakfast."

"Okay," Wylie said. "Go ahead and get dressed then."

Wylie laid back on the bed and watched Sheila change from her nightgown.

"Are you sure we can't play?" she asked.

"Positive."

"Bummer. Because now I'm hungry for something other than breakfast."

"Hold that thought," Sheila said.

"It's going to be a long day."

They went to a café and had pastries and coffee and chatted about the day ahead.

"So, it's going to be a long day on the bus today, isn't it?" Wylie said.

"Yes, but it will be very well worth it when the day is over."

"I'm really looking forward to seeing Karijini. I've read so much about it."

"You won't be disappointed," Sheila said.

They walked back to the hostel where everyone was ready and excited to hit the road. Wylie took her place, jittery with hormones in addition to looking forward to seeing the national park. She wished she'd had her way with Sheila that morning. She'd be feeling much better at the moment if she had. Still, she'd have her that night. If she could just calm down until then.

The bus made its way inland until they reached a small mining town where they stopped for lunch. Wylie was once again struck by the beauty of the red dirt all around. She and Sheila sat on a bench overlooking the river that wound its way through town. They enjoyed a leisurely lunch and then it was back on the bus for the last leg of the day. They finally stopped at the majestic Hamersley Range.

"Oh my God, it's beautiful," Wylie said to Sheila as she stepped off the bus.

"It is. And this is where we'll be camping tonight."

Wylie wandered about and took in the sight. There were high mountains surrounding her, and she was happy to know they'd have two whole days there for her to explore everything within eyesight and more.

The group went about setting up camp. Sheila set her area away from the others, for which Wylie was grateful, but she knew realistically she wouldn't have a chance to be with her for a couple of nights. She didn't know if the beauty of the area was worth the sacrifice.

After dinner, they had a bonfire, during which Wylie sat as close to Sheila as she could. Their thighs touched. It was torture, but she couldn't help herself. She had to be next to her, to touch her even if she couldn't touch her how she wanted to.

Chapter Five

Wylie woke with the sun and dressed quickly. She couldn't wait to explore. She set out on a short hike around the gorgeous Karijini National Park. She wandered down a gorge and took a quick dip in the river. It was chilly, and she felt refreshed after. She climbed back up and found the rest of the campers waking up. She was helping set up for breakfast when Sheila walked up.

"You're wet," she said.

"I always am around you," Wylie whispered.

"Aren't you funny? Seriously, where have you been?"

"I went for a swim in the river."

"Wylie! It's not safe to wander these areas alone. The terrain can be treacherous."

"I survived, right?

"Well, from now on, we'll do things together, okay? I don't want anything happening to you."

"Fair enough. I'll do things with you. Not the things I want to do, mind you, but things."

"You are so bad."

"And so good?"

"And so very good."

After breakfast, Wylie and Sheila set off on another adventure. They hiked through fields of wildflowers and watched birds flit about. They stood in awe at the rock formations that had been there for over two thousand years.

They found a trail to follow down to the bottom of the gorge. It led them to a swimming hole fed by a waterfall. They were alone, so they stripped naked and swam together in the cool water.

Wylie swam up next to Sheila and pulled her to her. She kissed her hard on the mouth as they treaded water.

"I've wanted to do that for so long," Wylie said.

"I love it when you do that."

They continued to kiss until Sheila finally pulled away.

"I need to be on solid ground."

"Fine," Wylie said. She swam behind the waterfall and sat on a rock ledge that had formed there. Sheila swam up and joined her.

They sat next to each other and kissed again. Each second the kiss became more passionate. Wylie couldn't contain herself. She ran her hand over Sheila's breast and teased the hard nipple she found there.

Sheila was breathing heavily and Wylie took that as a sign to keep going. She slid her hand lower until it rested on Sheila's thigh.

"I need you," she said.

"Take me."

Wylie slipped her fingers inside Sheila and moved them in and out while she pressed her palm against her clit. Sheila buried her face in Wylie's shoulder so her cry wouldn't be heard by everyone in the wilderness.

"That's what I'm talkin' about," Wylie said. "Now come on. Let's swim some more."

They swam for a few more minutes.

"I need to get back to camp and get lunch ready," Sheila said.

"Bummer."

"We have this afternoon and all of tomorrow to explore some more. Don't worry."

They hiked back to camp to find very few people there. Still, Sheila set out the packaged lunches for the rest of the group. She and Wylie sat with the others and ate their prepared lunches. They talked about what they'd done and seen that morning and soon others came back and joined them.

After a reasonable amount of time, though Wylie thought it was far too long, they said their good-byes to the others and set off again. They wandered along the edge of the gorge again, looking down at the multicolored rock and the pools of water.

"I can't get over this place. Travel guides don't do it justice," Wylie said.

"No. It's a little slice of heaven on earth."

They hiked and swam for the rest of the afternoon, then headed back to camp for dinner. Everyone was there, and they all spoke animatedly about the days they'd had. Wylie joined in, happy to have the camaraderie since she couldn't have Sheila. After dinner and the fire, she said good night to Sheila and climbed in to her sleeping bag where she quickly fell asleep, exhausted.

The next day was more of the same. Wylie and Sheila found their waterfall and swam and made love again. They hiked and took in all the area had to offer. When bedtime came that night, Wylie was sad to be leaving, but happy to be going to another hostel where she could properly take Sheila. It would be their last night together, and she planned to make it count.

The next morning everyone loaded up, excited for another day to explore, but people were getting antsy to get to Broome. Wylie was torn. She was excited to get to Broome, too, but she was sad to be saying good-bye to Sheila.

They headed back toward the coast that morning. They stopped at an iron ore port where they toured the town and had lunch. Wylie was once again taken aback by the sheer volume of iron mined in the region. After lunch, they drove to the Pilbara region where they would spend the last night of their tour.

The group ate their dinner in mixed tones. Some were happy this leg of their trip was over and they'd soon be moving on. Some were sad to say good-bye to the friends they had made along the way. Wylie and Sheila sat together in silence. Wylie was looking forward to bedtime.

"What's on your mind?" she finally asked.

"I always get a little melancholy at the end of a tour," Sheila said. "I can't help it."

"I can see that."

"And I'm more so this time."

"Yeah?"

"Yeah. Don't tell me you're not."

"Of course I am," Wylie said. "I'm excited to see Broome and all it has to offer, but I'm going to miss you. I'd be a liar if I said otherwise."

"I'm glad we have tonight. I'd be bummed if we ended our tour at a campsite. The past two nights have been hell."

"Tell me about it."

Sheila laughed.

"It's going to be rough getting back to not having sex all the time again."

"I'm sure you have more than your share of suitors," Wylie said.

"It's hard. Being on the road all the time. This was a special treat."

"Well, I've really enjoyed it, too."

People were putting their dinner dishes away. Wylie and Sheila joined them, then walked down to Sheila's room.

"Do you really think we're fooling anyone?" Wylie asked.

"I like to think so. And we could just have bonded really closely, you know."

"I suppose. I'd be suspicious."

"That's because you're you. You know what you'd be doing. There's no reason for anyone to suspect anything."

They closed the door behind them and Wylie stood in front of Sheila. She lightly ran her thumb over her cheek.

"This week really has been special. I want you to know that."

Sheila leaned into Wylie's palm and held her wrist.

"I want to believe that."

"Do."

She bent and took Sheila's lips with her own. She would miss these lips, these stolen moments. She pushed such thoughts out of her mind. It was time to focus only on the here and now. She needed to concentrate only on pleasing Sheila. And being pleased by her.

Sheila opened her mouth and Wylie slid her tongue inside. Again, she grew dizzy as their tongues rolled over each other. She fought to remain standing as she felt her knees tremble with desire. She pulled Sheila closer, as much to hold her up as to feel her pressed against her. The kiss deepened and Wylie finally had to pull away.

She slowly undressed Sheila, then quickly stripped out of her own clothes.

"Let's lie down," she said.

She took Sheila's hand and led her to the bed. Wylie kissed Sheila again. As hard as she could. She rolled on top of her and molded into her as they kissed. She ground her body into Sheila's until there was nothing, not even air, between them.

Wylie kissed down Sheila's cheek to her neck then back up to her mouth. She wanted every inch of her seared in her memory. She moved off her and ran her hand along her body, touching every inch she could see.

"I love your body." She knew she'd said it before, but it was true and she wanted Sheila to know she meant it.

"Thank you. I love yours."

Sheila ran her hand over Wylie's shoulders and arms.

"You're so strong. So sure of yourself," she said.

"I'm sure of what I want," Wylie said.

"What's that?"

"Oh, God," Wylie said. She kissed Sheila hard again and pinched an erect nipple. She slipped her hand between her legs and found her ready for her. She kissed down her body until she was between her legs.

"I found what I want," she said. She blew over the whole area and Sheila cried out.

"What are you doing?"

"Teasing you."

"It's working."

"You're so hot. I thought I'd cool you off a bit."

"No such luck," Sheila said.

"Good."

Wylie sucked on Sheila's lips and ran her tongue over and between them.

"You're delicious," she said.

She licked inside her and ran her tongue along her walls before she moved her mouth to her clit. She took it between her lips and sucked hard while she ran her tongue over its tip. Sheila had her hand on the back of Wylie's head, pressing her into her. She gyrated her hips in rhythm with Wylie's tongue.

Wylie felt Sheila tense against her as she called her name then collapsed on the bed.

Wylie climbed up next to her.

"Just a little something to remember me by," she said.

"I'll be thinking of you for a long time after tomorrow anyway," Sheila admitted. "But now I don't have to worry about getting laid for a while. I have no need after that."

They laughed together and Sheila let Wylie hold her while she caught her breath. When she could breathe normally again, she propped herself up on an elbow and looked into Wylie's eyes.

"And what would you like me to do to you?" she said.

"What do you mean?"

"I mean anything you want. Tell me. I'll do it for you. I want to make you feel as good as you made me feel."

Wylie laced her fingers behind her head.

"Take me. I don't care how. But I need relief and only you can give it to me. You don't need to do anything special. I promise."

Sheila kissed her then, on the mouth, before moving lower. She kissed down her chest and took a nipple deep in her mouth. She took half Wylie's small breast with it. She sucked as hard as she could and ran her tongue over the tip of the nipple.

Wylie tried to hold out but she couldn't. She whimpered as she reached a small orgasm.

"I'm not through with you," Sheila said.

She reached her hand down to where Wylie's legs met. Wylie spread her legs for her and Sheila stroked her hard clit. She moved lower and entered Wylie. She plunged her fingers deep inside. First two then three, deeper and deeper with each one. Wylie arched her hips and met each thrust.

Wylie thrashed her head on her pillow. She was so close. She needed to come. Dear God, she was close enough she could feel it was just a touch away. And that touch came, and with it, so did Wylie. It was one of the most powerful orgasms she'd ever had.

"Thank you for that," she said.

"My pleasure."

"I do believe it was mine." Wylie smiled.

She held her arm out and Sheila snuggled against her. They lay like that for a few minutes in silence.

"So what happens to you tomorrow?" Wylie said.

"I pick up a new group in Broome and do the same tour we just did only in reverse. And you? What are your plans in Broome?"

"I don't know. I plan to backpack around the region and check things out. I have the whole month off, so I might stay the whole time or I might not. We'll see. I should hang for a while then sign up for your tour back to Perth, huh?"

"You wouldn't know if I was the tour guide you'd get," she laughed.

"Ah, there is that. So I'll backpack around and maybe take an odd job or two for extra cash. It just depends."

"I admire your freedom," Sheila said.

"Don't you ever take vacations?"

"Sure I do. But not for a month at a time."

"Well, you should sometime."

"Maybe I will," Sheila said.

They lay together for a few more minutes before Wylie said the inevitable.

"I suppose I need to get going."

"I suppose you do."

"I don't want to."

"I don't want you to."

"So is this good-bye?" Wylie said.

"We'll say good-bye tomorrow, but it will be in a publically appropriate way."

"Got it."

Wylie got out of bed and dressed slowly. When all her clothes were on, Sheila climbed out of bed and crossed the room to her.

"Thank you for a wonderful week," she said.

"Thank *you*."

Sheila kissed Wylie hard on the mouth and Wylie pulled her close, reveling in the feel of her closeness one more time.

"I'll see you tomorrow," Wylie said, then let herself out.

Chapter Six

Wylie was awakened the next morning by the sound of her fellow travelers moving about. She stretched and checked her watch. She couldn't believe she hadn't been the first one up. But, she reasoned, she had been up late the night before. She smiled at the memory.

Breakfast was ready by the time she had loaded up her backpack. She found Sheila and sat next to her.

"How did you sleep?" she asked.

"Like a rock. You?"

"Me, too. I can't believe I just woke up. I was hoping for one more excursion before we set off."

"I told you it wasn't safe to hike alone," Sheila said. "So it's just as well you overslept."

The group did their breakfast dishes then climbed on the bus to set off to Broome. They stopped on the way for lunch at Eighty Mile Beach, an expanse of white sand and clear water the likes of which Wylie had never seen. They ate lunch and Wylie and Sheila went for a stroll along the sandy shore.

"This place is gorgeous," Wylie said.

"It is."

"I wish we had more time here. I see people fishing. I'd love to try my hand at that. Do you know what they're fishing for?"

"I'd imagine whiting and salmon."

"Yum."

"Yes, but what would you do if you caught one? You couldn't very well stuff it in your backpack until we get to Broome."

"I could release it."

"I suppose you could."

"I'm going to miss you, Sheila. I want you to know that."

"I'll miss you, too, Wylie. It's been a lot of fun."

"Yes, it has."

They turned around and wandered back up the beach to where the others were waiting. It had been a lovely break, but they still had a long drive to reach their destination.

They reached Broome just as the sun was setting. The orange glow it cast over the ocean made for excellent photographing as they got off the bus. This was it. The end of the road. People were hugging each other good-bye and promising to keep in touch. Phone numbers and email addresses were exchanged.

Wylie stood next to Sheila watching all of this.

"So, how about dinner tonight?" Wylie said.

"Are you sure? It would just prolong the inevitable."

"I suppose it would. But I have no plans and since you're in town, why not?"

"Okay. Let's go find a place."

They found an outdoor restaurant right on the water and sat drinking margaritas.

"A toast." Wylie raised her glass. "To life's adventures."

"Hear, hear." Sheila clinked her glass against Wylie's and they drank.

They ate steak and crab and got messy and laughed and really enjoyed their dinners. After, Sheila paid the bill with her tips from the tour.

"It's not necessary that you pay," Wylie had protested.

"I know. But I want to and I can. Let me."

"Yes, ma'am."

"So, I guess this really is good-bye. Unless you invite me to your room," Wylie said.

"I can't do that. As much as I'd love to. I have to get some sleep tonight. I have to get up early with a new tour tomorrow."

"Ah. I understand. Well, then, let me walk you to your hotel."

"Where are you staying?"

"At a hostel."

"Oh yeah. That makes sense. Okay. You can walk me to my room."

They strolled through the center of town until Sheila pointed out her hotel.

"So…" Wylie said.

"So."

"It's been fun."

"Lots."

"Take care of yourself, Sheila."

"You, too, Wylie."

"Good-bye."

"Good-bye."

Wylie kissed Sheila on her cheek and left her in search of her hostel.

Her hostel was located not far from Cable Beach, which looked like a beautiful place in the moonlight. Wylie was looking forward to exploring it more in the morning. She checked in at the counter.

"Hi. I'm Wylie Boase. I have reservations."

The young woman behind the counter looked her over. Wylie knew she was being checked out and wondered how interested the girl might be.

"So you do," the woman said. She took all Wylie's information and handed her a room key. "You have a private room, right?"

"That's correct."

The woman smiled at her.

"My name is Amarina. If there's anything I can do for you, please let me know."

Wylie flashed her a smile, one she knew showed off her dimples.

"I certainly will. Thank you."

Wylie started to her room. She passed a pool on the way. There were several people in and around it. She went back into the office and saw Amarina facing the other direction.

"Excuse me, Amarina?"

The woman turned to the desk.

"Yes?"

"What are the pool hours?"

"Nine in the morning until ten at night."

"That's good to know. I can take a moonlit dip tonight."

"Yes, you can. Enjoy."

"I will. Thank you."

Wylie hurried to her room and put her things away. She changed into her board shorts and T-shirt and headed to the pool. She only had a half an hour to swim, but it felt good to get wet after the long day on the bus.

She didn't speak to the others, as they all seemed to know each other and she would have felt like an intruder. She had plenty of time to get to know her new neighbors, she figured.

When it was ten o'clock, she climbed out and was drying off when a tall brunette walked up to her.

"You're new here, aren't you?"

"I am."

"I'm Kathryn."

"Nice to meet you. I'm Wylie."

"What brings you here?" Kathryn said.

"I'm going to do some backpacking."

"Great. This is a beautiful area to do it in. I've been doing that, too."

"Good to know."

"If you'd like, we could hike together tomorrow. I'm free if you are."

"That would be awesome. You can show me the sights."

"It would be my pleasure."

"What time would you like to meet up?" Wylie asked.

"How about eight? We could grab a cup of coffee and something to eat and then head out."

"Excellent. I'll see you then."

Wylie was up at seven, excited to spend her day sight-seeing with her new friend. She wandered out to the lobby by seven thirty and was sad to see that Amarina was nowhere to be seen. Oh well, she figured she must have time off, too. Even though Wylie had already set her sights on seducing her, she could be patient.

Kathryn walked up a few minutes later, looking quite attractive in shorts and a green safari shirt. The shirt brought out the green in her eyes and the shorts showed off tan, muscular legs. Wylie wondered if maybe she could get closer than she'd originally planned to her new friend.

"So, what are we doing first?" Wylie asked.

"I thought we'd hike around the gorges first and see some waterfalls. Then, this evening take a camel ride on the beach."

"Most excellent. I like the sound of it. But first, I need to buy you breakfast."

"I know just the place," Kathryn said.

They went to a small café that wasn't yet crowded. They found an outdoor table and chatted while they waited for their food.

"So, Kathryn, how long have you been here?"

"About a week. I've yet to grow tired of all the beauty in the area. But I'll be leaving in a few days, so I need to absorb as much of the exquisiteness as I can."

"Well, I'd hate to make you see something with me that you've already seen then. That doesn't seem fair to you," Wylie said.

"No. Really. I've seen it all. Now I get to see it through your eyes. I'm looking forward to that."

"Why me?" Wylie asked.

She noticed a slight redness creep under Kathryn's tan.

"Why not?"

"Fair enough. So, where are you from?"

"Boston."

"Wow. You're a long way from home."

"That I am."

"You born and raised there?"

"I grew up in Vermont, went to school in Boston, and stayed. What about you?"

"I live in a small town in Northern California. Same basic idea. Went to school there and stayed."

"So we have that in common."

"Yeah, we do."

After breakfast, they bought provisions, then set off on a hike to explore The Kimberley. Wylie followed behind Kathryn and enjoyed her tight ass as she walked along. They saw all sorts of bizarre rock formations, as well as deep pools of water and waterfalls. They'd been hiking for several hours and stopped by a waterfall for a break.

"I can't believe the wonder of this area," Wylie said.

"Isn't it beautiful?"

"It really is."

They ate their lunch in comfortable silence and when they were through, Kathryn stood and began to take her clothes off.

"What are you doing?" Wylie asked.

"I'm going swimming. It's too beautiful here not to."

"Do you have a suit?"

"No. Are you complaining?"

Of course Wylie wasn't complaining. She was just surprised at Kathryn's level of comfort with her.

"Not at all," she said.

"Come on, then. Let's get wet."

Wylie continued to watch until she was already wet and Kathryn was naked. Her perfectly toned body was tanned all over and Wylie itched to touch it. She told herself to calm down, that she didn't even know if Kathryn swung that way. She watched Kathryn step into the water before she finally stood and stripped herself.

The water was chilly, but not too cold, and it felt good after hiking in the dirt all those hours. She tried not to stare at Kathryn, but to focus on her surroundings. The top of the gorge was many feet up and the sheer rocks were a rusty red. The contrast of the rock walls with the blue water was magnificent.

Kathryn swam over to the waterfall and Wylie followed close behind. They swam under and around it and Wylie sat on a shelf behind it. The water there came up to her chest, so she didn't feel too exposed. And she wouldn't have to worry about temptation if Kathryn sat next to her. Which she did.

"I love looking out through waterfalls," Kathryn said.

"Yep. It just adds to the beauty of everything."

They sat there silently, with Wylie trying to focus on anything besides the nearness of Kathryn.

"What's on your mind?" Kathryn asked.

"Just enjoying the beauty of everything."

"Isn't nature amazing?"

"It truly is."

"So how'd you get so buff?" Kathryn said. "Are you a weightlifter or something?"

"I actually do manual labor for a living."

"Is that right? Good for you."

"Good for me?"

"Sure," Kathryn said. "I'm all for breaking stereotypes. A woman doing a man's job? Good for you."

"Thanks. I think."

"I mean it as a compliment."

"Okay. And what do you do?"

"I'm an executive vice president of a bank. It suits me."

"That's kind of a man's job, too, isn't it?"

Kathryn laughed.

"It used to be, but now the glass ceiling has been shattered. But manual labor? You don't see many women doing that. It certainly explains your body, though."

Wylie was becoming less comfortable by the moment. She was too close to an attractive naked woman for her liking, unless they were being intimate. And she felt like Kathryn was being condescending about her work.

"We should probably head back," Wylie said.

"We need to dry off before we get dressed."

"Oh. I didn't bring a towel."

"Neither did I. We'll just have to lay out to dry."

Great, Wylie thought. Lying next to Kathryn and not touching her would be close to hell. Although she was confused. Did she even want Kathryn? Yes, based on her body alone. The fact that she was smart and nice added to that. But her attitude about her job held her back. At any rate, did Kathryn want her? Who knew?

They spread out their clothes on the dirt and lay on top of them. Wylie was acutely and painfully aware of their closeness. She could roll over and touch Kathryn. She closed her eyes and tried not to think about it.

After a few minutes in the hot sun, they were dry enough to put their clothes back on. They dressed quickly and started back to their hostel.

"So, after the camel ride, how about dinner?" Kathryn asked.

Wylie thought about the question. How could there be any harm in that? Dinner still didn't mean anything.

"Sure. That would be great."

"It'll be my treat," Kathryn said.

"No. I'll pay for it." Wylie wasn't used to her dates paying for the meal.

"I insist. I asked, so I pay."

"Fair enough."

"And after dinner, perhaps a nightcap by the pool?"

"Sure. Sounds great. Where does one find a nightcap in a hostel?"

Kathryn laughed.

"We'll have to hit the liquor store to buy whatever we'll want to drink."

"Ah. Got it."

They returned to the hostel just before sunset. They stowed away their hiking gear then met in the lobby to go ride the camels. Amarina was there, and Wylie wished she was by herself so she could talk to the cute blonde. Instead, she gave her a quick hello and good-bye and went down to the beach with Kathryn.

The ride was quite an adventure. Camels are not like horses, as Wylie quickly learned. She sat in front and Kathryn sat behind her. She felt like she was ten feet off the ground and fought her fear of falling off. The camels were sure-footed on the white sands though, and soon she relaxed into it and went with the flow and was able to enjoy all she was seeing.

The reflection of the sun off the water was stunning to see, but the way the light played off the red cliffs in the distance was breathtaking. This was a once in a life time experience, and Wylie once again committed every aspect of it to memory.

After the ride, Wylie let Kathryn choose a restaurant since she was paying for dinner. She chose a nice one with a covered patio that looked out over the water.

"This is a nice place," Wylie said.

"Thanks. I haven't tried it yet, so I make no promises. But I've had my eye on it since I got here."

"Fair enough. We'll check it out together."

They ordered margaritas as they looked over the menu. They decided on dinner and after they ordered, sat back to enjoy the view.

"What a day," Wylie said. "Thank you for being my tour guide."

"My pleasure." Kathryn smiled. "Weren't those camels marvelous?"

"Oh my God. I never realized how big they are. I was terrified up there."

"So was I when I first got on. Then you kind of relax into it, don't you?"

"Exactly."

They kept their conversation light and friendly as they ate and, after dinner, took a leisurely stroll to the liquor store where they bought tequila, margarita mix, and glasses and wandered back to the hostel. They went to their respective rooms and changed into their suits. They met back at the pool.

"I love your look," Kathryn said.

"Yeah. I don't feel comfortable in your basic woman's suit."

"You wouldn't look right in it."

"Thanks. I think."

"It was a compliment. Sometimes I think you don't trust when I compliment you."

"How so?"

"Right there was an example," Kathryn said. "And when I told you how awesome I think your job is."

"Maybe you're right. I'm sorry. I'll try not to be so defensive."

"There you go."

They sat by the pool drinking their margaritas, occasionally dipping in the water to cool off. The evening was warm, made warmer, Wylie thought, by Kathryn's presence. She was a beauty, to be sure. And the way she filled out her bikini made Wylie's mouth water. Her breasts were full and firm, and her ass was tight. Wylie longed to take her to bed.

When ten o'clock rolled around and it was time to leave the pool, they gathered their things.

"Okay, either you're not interested, insanely shy, or I've lost my touch," Kathryn said.

"What do you mean?"

"I mean, you've done nothing to indicate you're interested in me. You've been polite and fun, but you haven't touched me or anything like that. You haven't flirted at all. And here I feel like I've been throwing myself at you."

Wylie couldn't help but laugh.

"I had no idea. I find you very attractive, Kathryn, but I didn't know if you were on my team."

"Well, I am. And if you don't take me to bed tonight, I think I'll self-combust."

Chapter Seven

W ell, we wouldn't want that to happen," Wylie said. "I'm glad to hear that."

"So, come on. Let's go to my room."

They walked along the outside of the hostel until they came to Wylie's room. She was surprised to notice her hand shaking as she tried to get the key in the hole. She had nothing to be nervous about. Kathryn was a beautiful and willing playmate. Life was good.

She got the door open and stood aside to let Kathryn enter. There wasn't a lot of space in her little room, so they had to stand somewhat close to each other. Wylie still felt unsure of herself. She didn't know what was up. She took a deep breath.

"Would you like another drink?" she asked.

"No, thanks. I think I've had enough."

Wylie moved in close to Kathryn. Close enough to smell the chlorine in her hair. She loved that smell. She nuzzled her neck before kissing her lightly on her mouth. The hormonal response inside her was immediate. She kissed her harder and was happy when that kiss was returned in kind.

She reached behind Kathryn and untied her bikini top. Her full breasts stood free for her taking. Wylie stood admiring them for a moment before she took them in her hands and held them. She kissed Kathryn again as she ran her hands over her breasts. She dragged her thumbs over her nipples and felt them tighten at her touch.

Wylie bent down and took a nipple in her mouth while she pinched and tugged on the other one. She moved her hand down Kathryn's taut stomach and ran her fingertips just under the waist of her bottoms. She felt her shiver in anticipation. Wylie was wet with anticipation of her own.

"Get me out of these," Kathryn said. "Please."

Wylie walked Kathryn back to the bed. She peeled off her bikini bottoms.

"Now, lie down," Wylie said.

Kathryn did as instructed. She lay there watching Wylie undress. This was a major turn on for Wylie. She loved to be watched. When she was naked, she joined Kathryn on the bed.

She ran her hand over the length of her, surprised at how soft and smooth her skin was.

"You really take care of yourself," Wylie said.

"I have good genes."

Wylie buried her face in Kathryn's neck and nipped and nuzzled it as her hand moved lower until it came to rest between her legs. She stroked her lightly, which drove them both crazy.

"Please," Kathryn said. "I've wanted this since I saw you last night. Please don't tease me."

Wylie just laughed and kept up her slow stroking. Kathryn was so wet. She felt so good. Wylie didn't want to rush anything.

"Dear God, woman," Kathryn said. "What are you waiting for?"

Wylie kissed down her neck and chest again and drew a nipple deep in her mouth. She did this at the same time she began to rub Kathryn's clit. The combination proved too much for Kathryn and she grabbed hold of Wylie's wrist as she came.

Wylie kissed her mouth again and lightly pulled her wrist away from Kathryn's death grip.

"Thank you for that," Kathryn said.

"Thank you. I enjoyed it very much."

Kathryn slid her hand between Wylie's legs.

"I'd say you did," she said. "You're about as wet as anyone I've ever felt."

Wylie wondered just how many women Kathryn had felt, but decided she didn't need to know.

Kathryn didn't tease. She plunged her fingers inside Wylie and kept them there. Then she slowly withdrew them before thrusting them in again.

Wylie was in heaven. She liked to be fucked hard and fast, and Kathryn was right on target. She tried to hold off as long as she could, but it was no use. The pressure built in her center and soon exploded, sending waves of orgasms cascading over her body.

They lay together in silence for a few minutes.

"Are you going to kick me out?" Kathryn said.

"Not if you don't want to go. You're welcome to stay the night with me."

"I'd like that."

Kathryn settled into Wylie's arms and they both fell sound asleep.

The next morning, Kathryn went back to her room to shower and change before they started their day. They met in the lobby. Wylie got there first to find Amarina behind the desk.

"Do they ever give you time off?" she asked, even though she knew the answer.

Amarina smiled at her.

"Sometimes. I don't mind working. It gives me something to do."

Wylie's heart skipped a beat at her dimpled smile and mussed blond hair. She thought how nice it would be to wake up next to her after a night of lovemaking.

"There's so much to do around here. Do you ever play tourist?"

"Not as often as I'd like."

"Well, maybe someday we can play tourist together," Wylie said.

"That would be nice."

"Great."

Just then Kathryn walked up.

"I hope I'm not interrupting anything," she said.

"Not at all. I was just chatting with Amarina here."

"Are you ready for our day?"

"I am." She waved good-bye to Amarina. "I'll see you later."

"So, you sure you'll be okay with just a day on the beach?" Kathryn asked.

"Sure I'm sure. We'll grab some beer and just kick back and swim all day. I'd like to try to do some fishing, too."

"They have charter boats that go out. Would you rather do that?"

"Maybe tomorrow. Today, let's just be lazy."

"I won't do the chartered trip with you," Kathryn said. "I get horribly sea sick."

"No lie?"

"No lie."

"Okay, well, maybe I will do that this afternoon then."

They walked along the beach, past the north access road to where the beach was clothing optional. They both stripped and got in the turquoise water, which was warm yet refreshing. They swam and frolicked and chased each other in the waves. They simply enjoyed themselves, which was what they had agreed to do that day.

After several hours, they put their clothes back on and walked back toward town. They said their good-byes after they promised to meet for dinner that night and Wylie headed to a local charter fishing company.

She was lucky as a boat was leaving right then to take a group of fishermen to the fishing vessel. She paid and got in. The ride was quick and she was excited to try her hand. She'd only fished in rivers and lakes and had no idea how she'd fare in the ocean. But she couldn't wait to try.

They arrived at the big boat, a nice one with lots of covered space to stay cool. But Wylie wasn't afraid of the sun and the heat. She already had a dark tan, but she wasn't a fool. She applied her sunscreen and trusted Mother Nature to do the rest.

She was given a rod, then a man came by with a bait bucket. It was mostly fish heads. It didn't smell very good to her, but she hoped some big fish would find it too good to pass up. She cast her line far out into the ocean, then sat down to wait. As she waited, a young man brought around beers and offered her one. She took one gratefully and sipped it as she watched her line.

The boat rocked gently in the waves which could have lulled her to sleep if she allowed it to. There was occasional talking, but for the most part, people were silent as they watched their lines just like her. No one had had a bite in a couple of hours and Wylie was just about to consider her day a wash when the tip of her line dipped low into the water. She grabbed her pole and pulled it out of its holder.

"Keep the tip up," one of the crew members said to her.

There were three of them by her side, all talking at once.

"Do you need help?" another said.

"Be patient."

"I don't think I need help," Wylie said, though she wasn't really sure.

She tried to be patient, but after fighting the fish for ten minutes, her arms were getting sore. She kept the tip up and kept trying to reel it in, but it kept swimming back out. She kept up the fight, though, and soon the fish was close enough to the boat for them to see it was a nice sized tuna.

"Just a little more," one of the men said.

She kept at it and finally lifted it to the edge of the boat and into the waiting net of one of the crew.

"She's a beauty."

Wylie was winded and sore, but was all smiles. Pictures were taken of her with her catch and then the men offered to cook it for her. She couldn't stand the idea of killing such a wondrous beast.

"Let's release her," she said.

The men looked at each other.

"Are you serious?"

"I am. I caught her. I have proof. Let's let her go."

"Hey. The customer's always right, eh?" one of the men said.

Wylie just smiled. She stood back and watched as they tossed the fish back into the water. She sat back and drank beer the rest of the afternoon, too sore to even contemplate another fight like the one the tuna had put up.

When she was back on solid ground, she walked back to the hostel. She was looking forward to a hot shower and change of clothes. Amarina was still working. She took one look at Wylie.

"You look beat."

"I am, but it was well worth it."

"Where have you been? And where's Kathryn? I thought she went with you."

"We spent the morning at the beach, but then I went fishing. I caught a five-and-a-half-foot tuna."

She pulled out her phone and showed Amarina a picture.

"Oh wow! That's a big fish."

"It was."

"Did you have it for lunch, then?"

"No, I had them throw it back."

"That was very decent of you. Thank you for doing that."

"Of course," Wylie said. "I couldn't possibly eat that much. Nor do I know enough people to share it with. And it was too beautiful and deserved to live another day."

"What are your plans now?" Amarina said.

"I'm taking a shower then meeting Kathryn for dinner."

"Oh," Amarina said.

"Yep, so I better get to it."

"Well, have fun."

"I'll talk to you later."

Wylie showered and dressed quickly and hurried to the lobby to meet Kathryn. She was a little early, but hoped that meant she would have more time to talk to Amarina. But Kathryn was early, too, so they just set off for dinner.

Dinner was another pleasant experience, and afterward, they went back to Wylie's room.

"So, when do you leave?" Wylie asked.

"I leave the day after tomorrow. So I've kind of committed myself to spend tomorrow with the group I came with."

"Oh, okay," Wylie said. "That makes sense."

She would have loved more time with the lovely Kathryn, but a couple of nights of sex with her were better than none.

"Well then," she continued, "We'd better make the most out of tonight."

She kissed Kathryn hard on her mouth as she fumbled with the zipper down the back of her sundress. She finally got it down and Kathryn stepped out of the dress. She unhooked her bra and slid her panties off, leaving herself bare for Wylie's pleasure.

Wylie ran her hands all over her body, finally resting them on her ass and pressing her pelvis into her own.

"You need to get undressed," Kathryn said.

Wylie quickly complied and took Kathryn in her arms once again. As they kissed, Wylie's passion flared. Soon, she could no longer stand. She pulled Kathryn to the bed and laid her down.

She climbed on top of her and dragged her knee up to press it against her. She placed her hand over it and plunged her fingers deep inside. She used her knee to give her an extra push as she continued to move in and out. She moved her hand to Kathryn's clit and rubbed until Kathryn cried out as she climaxed.

Kathryn reached between Wylie's legs, but Wylie stopped her.

"Why not?" Kathryn asked.

"I'm exhausted. Come here and let me hold you."

Kathryn stood and grabbed her clothes.

"I should get going," she said.

"Kathryn, look…"

"No. It's all good. I just need to get up early tomorrow."

"I'm sorry. I'm tired," Wylie said.

"That's okay. Honest. Don't worry about it." Kathryn bent over and kissed Wylie hard on the mouth.

"It's been nice knowing you," she said.

"Yeah. You, too. Have a safe trip home."

"You, too."

And Kathryn was gone. Wylie fell into a deep sleep and awoke the next day feeling like a million bucks. She walked into the lobby to see Amarina working. She flashed her a bright smile.

"Good morning, Amarina," she said.

"Hello." Her response seemed cool.

"How are you this morning?"

"Fine."

"Hey," Wylie said. "Are you okay?"

"I said I'm fine. Now, is there something I can help you with?"

Wylie was confused. She didn't know if the attraction was mutual, but she'd at least thought they both enjoyed flirting. So what was up with Amarina that morning? She decided not to worry about it at the moment.

"Hey, I'm still beat after yesterday," she said. "Do you know where one rents quads to ride around?"

"Go out the front door and it's two blocks that way."

She pointed right.

"Thanks a lot," Wylie said.

She got no response. She gave Amarina a questioning look, but got a defiant stare in return, so she headed out to start her day.

She rented a four-runner and started out the opposite way that she and Kathryn had hiked. She wanted to see more of the area. The gorges were beautiful and the water inviting. But she didn't swim. Not that day. She just rode around exploring all there was to see. She returned to Broome late that afternoon. She took the quad back then headed back to the hostel. She was covered in dust and couldn't wait to jump in the pool. She walked into the lobby and Amarina was still there.

"Hey you," Wylie said.

Amarina looked up from her work.

"Oh, hi."

"How was your day?"

"Fine."

She didn't bother to ask how Wylie's was, which didn't escape Wylie at all. Something was up and she really wanted to get to the bottom of it.

"So what time do you get off today?" Wylie said.

"Six."

"Would you like to have dinner then? That gives me time to shower and get decent."

"No, thanks."

"You sure? My treat."

"I'm sure."

Amarina walked back behind the deck and pulled a piece of paper from Wylie's room slot.

"This is for you," Amarina said.

"Thanks. And we were going to play tourist together. How about tomorrow?"

"I work."

"Okay, well, I'll see you later then." Wylie felt uncomfortable. Something was up with Amarina, and Wylie had no idea what it was. She got to her room and unfolded the piece of paper Amarina had handed her.

Wylie,
Thanks for the past few days. I had a great time with you. And the nights were magical. I'll miss you.

It then listed her phone number and email address.

Wylie looked at the note. She contemplated throwing it away. She would never need Kathryn's phone number or email address. But she thought better of it and tossed it in her backpack. Someday she might be in Boston. Maybe she'd look her up. Who knew?

Wylie quickly changed into her swim outfit and hit the pool. There were several people there, but Wylie kept to herself. She swam a few laps then got out and headed to her room. She showered and dressed for dinner. She stopped by the lobby right at six to see if she could convince Amarina to go with her, but she was already gone.

Bummer, Wylie thought, and set off for dinner alone.

CHAPTER EIGHT

The following morning, Wylie was up with the sun, ready to start a new day. She had decided to explore Malcolm Douglas Wilderness Park. She was excited to see what kinds of wildlife she might stumble upon. She was going to go on her own, but decided it might be safer with a tour, so she found one that departed nearby and bought a ticket. The tour left at two, which meant she had several hours to kill.

She headed back to the hostel and changed into her swim attire then headed for the beach. She stopped in the lobby to see if Amarina was in a better mood, but she wasn't there.

"What time does Amarina work today?" she asked.

"Today is her day off."

So it hadn't been Wylie's imagination. Amarina was pissed at her. Why else would she have told her a blatant lie? But for what? She'd have to find out and make it right.

She walked to the beach and swam in the beautiful water. She alternated swimming and lying out. Her tan had deepened by several degrees, which made her very happy. She knew she had to be careful of overexposure, but she was. She used sunscreen all the time. The last thing she wanted was a sunburn to impede her fun.

She went back to the hostel and put her clothes on then went to the departure site and waited for the bus.

It finally arrived and she sat back and relaxed on the fifteen-minute ride to the park. The tour wasn't quite full, which meant more time for everyone to explore. Wylie stopped and got her picture taken in the giant fiberglass head of a crocodile that is the entrance to the park. The picture turned out wonderfully, and she bought it as soon as she saw it. She knew it was all part of the tourist trap, but didn't care. How many people did she know who'd ever stood in the mouth of a crocodile, real or not?

Once inside the park, the tour guide took them past pools of crocodiles of several different species. They even had American crocodiles. Wylie was glad she'd brought her good camera. There was so much to see and she wanted to document everything on film.

She particularly enjoyed the colorful birds that they saw all over the place, especially the cassowary. She kept her distance, but took several pictures of it. She enjoyed all the wildlife she saw, like the dingoes, which looked like regular dogs, but she knew better than to get too close. She even saw a rare black and white dingo, so she shot several photos of that one.

Everything she saw was beautiful and amazing to her. She saw wallabies and kangaroos. Wallabies and kangaroos just hanging out and being themselves. She couldn't believe her eyes. There were other creatures she'd never heard of before, but she photographed them to capture them in history.

And then there was the feeding of some of the largest crocodiles in captivity. They would leap from the water to take the bait and Wylie's heart jumped every time. They were massive animals, and she knew the damage they could do. Even though they were trained individuals who fed them, it was hard not to jump in fear.

Another part of the tour Wylie fully enjoyed was the snake show. She got to hold a long, black snake that wrapped around her. She could feel how powerful it was, but she wasn't scared. An experienced snake handler stood right next to her, ready to help if things got out of control. But they didn't. She had someone take a picture with her phone and then passed the snake on to someone else.

Wylie was feeling very good as they boarded the bus back to Broome. She had seen so much and learned so much. It was a great feeling. She got off the bus in Broome and wandered through the quaint little town looking for somewhere to eat. She found a burger joint and went in. She had a burger and fries and washed it all down, as well as the dust of the day, with several beers.

She went back to the hostel and swam for a bit before climbing into bed, exhausted again.

Wylie realized she was slowly but surely falling in love with the small town of Broome and its surrounding areas. She started thinking seriously about maybe getting a job at the Wilderness Park. Or as a hand on one of the fishing boats. She really thought she might like to stay a while.

The next morning, she went to the lobby to see if Amarina was around. Sure enough, there she sat behind the desk.

"Hey, Amarina. How are you today?"

Amarina looked up, then back down.

"Fine."

"Look, Amarina," Wylie said. "Obviously I've done something to upset you. I don't know what it could be. But if you tell me, I won't do it again. I promise. And I'll even do my best to make it up to you."

"What do you care anyway?" Amarina asked. "I'm a desk clerk at a hostel you're staying at for a couple of weeks."

"Because when I first walked in here, you seemed like a really nice person. You even agreed to go sight-seeing with me. Then you changed your tune. You're borderline rude to me. And I don't know why."

"I don't know what you mean."

"Sure you do."

"Look, Wylie Boase. I'm not some Kathryn that you can play with for a while and then let go."

Wylie was dumbfounded. Yes, she had wanted to take Amarina to bed, but only if it was mutual. She hadn't seen this response coming at all. And how had she known about Kathryn? Then she remembered the note.

"Okay. So I won't treat you that way. But can't we at least be friends?"

"I'm not usually friends with players."

"I'm not really a player." Wylie might have been stretching the truth a little there. "And I would never do anything to hurt you. I like you. I want to get to know you better. Is there anything wrong with that?"

Wylie watched Amarina closely. She seemed to relax a little bit.

"I don't know. I don't know that I trust you."

"You don't even know me," Wylie said. "Right? How can you know if you trust me if you won't take a chance and get to know me?"

Amarina sat silently, as if weighing her options.

"Look," Wylie said. "I'm sorry if I came on too strong to you in the beginning."

"You seemed to really like me. But you were sleeping with Kathryn."

"Would it matter if I said she seduced me?" Wylie said.

"I wouldn't believe you."

"Fair enough. So let's start from the beginning. From before Kathryn."

"Fine. But how do I know you're not bedding someone else now?"

"I'm not," Wylie said, though she was unsure what business it was of Amarina. She was just glad she could say it honestly. "So, how about dinner tonight? What time do you get off work?"

"Five."

"I'll be here."

"Okay." Amarina still sounded hesitant.

"You'll see," Wylie said. "I'm not an ogre."

Wylie was about to leave, when she saw a help wanted notice on the bulletin board. It was for pearl diving. She had never been, but was PADI certified in SCUBA diving, so felt she might have a chance at it. And it would allow her to stay in Broome a little longer. She took one of the fliers attached to it and left the lobby.

She studied the address, then realized she had no idea where it was. She walked back into the lobby.

"Hey, Amarina?"

"Yes?"

"Can you tell me where this is?" She handed the flier to her.

"What do you need to know for?"

"I'm thinking of taking a job. I'd love to stay here longer, and I think this would be a good job for me."

"It's a lot of hard work, or so I've heard," Amarina said.

"I'm not afraid of hard work, so no worries there."

Amarina gave her directions and Wylie set off to find the office of the pearl diving company. She found it just where Amarina had said it would be. The place smelled of fish and salt water. She walked in and approached the desk where a middle-aged woman sat, typing on her keyboard.

"Hello," Wylie said.

The woman jumped.

"Sorry," Wylie said. "I didn't mean to startle you."

"It's okay. I was just lost in thought. What can I do for you?"

"I'm here to see about a job."

"You are, are you?"

"Yes, ma'am."

"Please, no 'ma'am.' I'm not that old."

Wylie laughed. The woman had spunk; she had to give her that.

"You can just call me Nadine."

"Great. So, about that job?"

"Oh, yeah. Here's an application to fill out." She handed Wylie a clipboard and a pen. "I have to say, it's a tough job. You ever done any hard work?"

"I'm a brick layer," Wylie said.

"Okay then. That'll probably do. Anyway, fill this out and bring it back to me."

Wylie sat on the bench and filled out the forms. The only thing she didn't have was her PADI certificate, but she figured she could bring it later. She looked over the application and felt good about it. She walked back up to the desk, but Nadine was on the phone. So she sat back down and waited.

When Nadine was off the phone, Wylie brought her application back to the desk.

"Oh, hon," she said. "You could have just left it here. You didn't need to wait."

"I wasn't sure if there was more," Wylie said.

"Nope. You left us your number?" She flipped to the back page. "Great. We'll get in touch with you."

Wylie walked out of the office and was happy to be in the fresh air. Though, she supposed she'd better get used to the smell of fish if she was going to work on a pearl diving vessel.

She walked down the seaside street until she came to the same burger joint where she'd had dinner the night before. She enjoyed a leisurely lunch, then walked along the beach until she arrived at the clothing optional area. There were a few people there already, but she wasn't shy about her body. She stripped down and got in the water. It felt amazing. It was a hot day and it felt good to get wet.

Wylie alternated swimming and lying out in the sun for several hours before finally getting dressed and heading back to the hostel. She didn't want to be late for dinner. She dug through her bag and found a clean pair of cargo shorts and a black golf shirt. She knew she'd be warm in the black shirt, but it was clean and looked good on her, both necessary. She knew she had to keep it mellow that evening. She couldn't flirt per se, but she could subtly charm Amarina. And that's what she intended to do. She wanted to get back into Amarina's good graces. She didn't like that her time with Kathryn may have blown her chances with Amarina. Kathryn had been fun, but Amarina called to her. She drew her to her like few women ever had. She wanted to get to know her better. That was for sure.

She arrived in the lobby at five o'clock on the dot. There was no sign of Amarina.

"Excuse me," Wylie said to the man behind the counter. "Do you know where Amarina is?"

"Not a clue. She called and asked me to come in an hour early, so I did. She left around four. I've no idea why."

Wylie fought not to let her disappointment show. She left the lobby and heard a car door slam. She turned to see Amarina standing there. She was dressed in a white dress with red polka dots on it.

Her hair was held back from her face by a red headband. She looked adorable.

"Hey you," Wylie said when she finally found her voice.

"Where you goin'?"

"I figured you blew me off, so I was just leaving."

"Don't you know it's a lady's prerogative to be late?"

Wylie laughed.

"True. Very true. I'm sorry. You just told me you worked until five, then I came by at five and he tells me you left at four...well, surely you can see from my point of view that it looked like you were avoiding me."

"I suppose it could have looked that way. But it wasn't. I'm here now."

"And you look beautiful," Wylie said.

"Thank you."

"So, do you mind walking? I know of a great restaurant right up the street."

"I've been to most of the places around here. I don't mind oceanfront dining at all."

"Great." She let Amarina walk first and took her place on the outside of the sidewalk as they walked to the restaurant.

"This place is real expensive," Amarina said. She hesitated at the door and started to back away. Wylie placed her hand on her back.

"Don't worry about it. It's my treat, anyway." She opened the door and they walked into the refreshingly air conditioned building.

"Did you want to sit outside or inside?" Amarina said.

"I'd love to sit on the patio and look at the water, but it sure feels good inside. Do you have a preference?"

"I'll always choose outside if given a choice."

"Okay then, outside it will be."

The hostess seated them and they studied their menus. Wylie searched her mind for something to say. Something clever or witty.

"The steak and crab legs is a really good choice," she said lamely.

"Really? That just seems so messy."

Wylie bit her tongue and said nothing about getting messy with Amarina, though the idea was definitely forefront in her mind. It wasn't going to happen that night, though, so she told herself to keep her hormones in check for the time being. It wouldn't be easy after spending an evening with the beauty in front of her, but she'd do her best.

"Messy just means fun," Wylie said. "It's what I'm having so I hope I don't gross you out."

"You're going to get that? Really? Okay, if you get it I get it. We can get messy together."

Wylie tried not to laugh but was unsuccessful. What could she say? She had the mind of a twelve-year-old boy sometimes.

"That we will," she said, hoping the laughter went unnoticed.

"Was that so funny, then?" Amarina said.

Wylie tried to backpedal.

"I'm sorry. It just sounded…"

"It's okay. I'm just picking on you. It did sound suggestive. I knew it as soon as it came out of my mouth. As long as you know that's the only way we'll be getting messy together tonight."

"Fair enough," Wylie said. She couldn't wipe the smile off her face. This one had spunk. There was no denying it. And she liked it. A lot.

They ordered their dinners and sat back to watch the sunset.

"So, how did you end up working at a hostel in Broome?" Wylie asked.

"I was born and raised here. My father works on the charter fishing boats. I went off to university to study the hospitality industry. My hope was to get a job at a hotel or resort around here. But the only job available was at the hostel. I've worked my way up to manager and I love my job, so you won't hear me complaining."

"Well, I'm glad you got the job. If you hadn't, what would you have done?"

"I don't know. I don't even like to think about it. Most likely get a job at a hotel in another town, but Broome is my home. It's where I need to be."

"So, are you pretty close to your parents?" Wylie said.

"Very. As are my brothers and sisters. We're a very close-knit family. What about you?"

"My folks disowned me."

Amarina reached across the table and took Wylie's hand with her own.

"I'm so sorry to hear that. That's got to be unbearable."

"It is what it is," Wylie said. "They're a good Catholic family and couldn't handle their daughter being a lesbian."

"That's what scares me," Amarina said. "I don't know what my family would do if they found out."

"I didn't know what to expect, but they wanted nothing to do with me."

"Nothing? Really?"

"Really. I stayed in the closet for a long time. All through high school and college. But once I started working, I came out to them and they said I wasn't welcome in their home anymore."

"I'm sorry." She squeezed Wylie's hand. Wylie loved having her hand held by Amarina. Her hands were soft and gentle and Wylie imagined holding one on a walk on the beach.

"It's been several years now. I've made friends and have coworkers who I consider family. I'm never alone on holidays or anything like that. I really consider it my family's loss."

"I'm glad. I would be sad to think of you alone on holidays. Although you're traveling alone here."

"Oh sure. I take my vacations by myself. I meant holidays like Christmas and Thanksgiving and such. I forget you guys call vacations holidays."

"Yes, we do. I see what you mean now. That's good. Your family made a terrible decision to disown you, I think."

"Even though I'm a player?" Wylie smiled.

Amarina blushed.

"Even though."

Dinner arrived and the conversation kept up.

"So, you went to college, too, huh?" Amarina said.

"I did. I graduated, too."

"And what are you doing for a living?"

"I'm a brick layer."

"Really? They teach that in college in the United States?"

"No." Wylie laughed. "I was working doing that part-time while I went to school. I really liked the small town the college was in and wanted to stay there. So, I went full-time and the rest is history."

"That sounds like a lot of hard work."

"It is. But hey, it saves me the cost of a gym membership."

"I'm sure it does."

Amarina fidgeted with her dress. Wylie wondered why she seemed uncomfortable all of a sudden.

"What's up?" she asked.

"Nothing." Amarina wouldn't lift her gaze from her lap.

"Was it something I said?"

"No. It's not you. It's just that sometimes..."

"What? Talk to me Amarina. I'm a good listener."

"Sometimes I get embarrassed that my body isn't perfect."

"Nonsense, Amarina. You've got a wonderful body."

"See? You're supposed to say that."

"No. I'm not. But if I thought there was something wrong with your body would I ever have flirted with you in the first place?"

"I don't know."

"The answer is no. I wouldn't have. I like that you're not all skin and bones. I mean that."

"Yeah?"

"Yeah. Now finish your dinner and maybe we can go for a walk on the beach?"

"That would be great."

"Right on. So, eat up."

CHAPTER NINE

After dinner they took a casual stroll along the beach. The night was warm, but comfortable. They took their shoes off and walked in the water.

"Do you ever think you take this for granted?" Wylie asked.

"How do you mean?"

"I mean, you've lived here your whole life. Do you still realize how breathlessly beautiful this place is? Or is it just home to you?"

"Oh no. I love how gorgeous it is. I love everything the area has to offer, but Broome is a very special place. The people, the sights. Everything about it makes it unique."

"Good. I was afraid you wouldn't still take the time to breathe in its magic every once in a while."

"That will never happen."

"So, what happened to our day of sight-seeing together? Can we still do that?" Wylie asked. She was really enjoying her time with Amarina and wanted more of it.

"I suppose it wouldn't hurt."

"Thank you?"

"I'm still not sure about you and your motives."

"Then let me be clear. I find you to be a very attractive woman, Amarina. Both physically and otherwise. I want to get to know you better. That's it in a nutshell."

"Hm. I appreciate that."

"But you're hesitant," Wylie said.

"No. I'm a bit disappointed."

"How so?" Wylie was confused. She was doing all she knew how to be the perfect gentlewoman with Amarina.

"Well, a player like you isn't interested in bedding me? That's not too good for the ego."

Wylie laughed. It was a deep belly laugh that she couldn't control.

"I just can't win, can I?" she said. "I'm not a player. I told you."

"So you've no interest in taking me to bed?"

"That's such a double-edged sword. There's no right answer." She paused. "Okay. I'll be honest. I'd love to take you to bed. But I'd love to get to know you first. How's that?"

"That makes me feel a little better."

Wylie laughed again. She really liked Amarina. A lot. And she was willing to be as patient as she had to be before making love to her. However, if Amarina needed her to take her to bed to prove her affection, she'd be happy to do that. More than happy.

They had walked far enough and Amarina suggested they turn around and head back.

"So about that sight-seeing day?" Wylie tried again.

"Oh, yeah. Let's do it tomorrow. I took the day off."

"You did, huh?"

"Yes. And I talked to my brother. He has a small plane and he's agreed to fly us out over the gorge."

"You've already taken care of everything, huh?"

"I did. I rather thought you'd want to spend tomorrow together, regardless of how tonight ends."

"And how will tonight end?" Wylie said.

"I haven't decided."

Wylie smiled to herself. So there was hope.

They walked the rest of the way in silence, with Wylie's hormones in overdrive. She really wanted Amarina and her hinting she may have a chance with her that night had her boxers more than a little damp.

When they arrived at the hostel, Wylie walked Amarina to her car.

"You may as well get in," Amarina said.

"Don't sound so excited."

"I don't know if I'm doing the right thing."

"Then I tell you what. Let's hold off."

"But that's the thing. I don't want to."

Wylie opened the door and climbed in.

"We don't have to do anything, you know," she said. "I could just hold you."

"That's not what my body wants."

"Well, we definitely should give your body what it wants."

They drove to Amarina's house. Wylie checked out the sights as they drove, since she'd spent most of her time on the beachfront. They arrived at a small bungalow and Amarina announced they were there.

"This is the cutest place I've ever seen," Wylie said.

"Thank you. It's not much, but it's home."

They walked inside and Wylie felt like she'd gone back decades in time. Strands of beads served as doorways and lava lamps lit the rooms.

"I think you were born in the wrong generation," Wylie said.

"Ya think?"

"I love your place, though. It's got such a homey feel to it."

"Thanks," Amarina said. "It's my private sanctuary. Very few people get to see it."

"Really?"

"Really. Oh, sure, my family have all been here, but few other people."

"You really keep to yourself, huh?"

"Well, the hostel keeps me so busy, you know? And I meet so many people there. That I don't really have time for a social life outside of there."

Wylie crossed the room and stood in front of Amarina. She fingered the ends of Amarina's hair.

"You don't have time for one or you don't want one?"

Amarina reached up and placed her hand over Wylie's.

"I like all the people I meet at the hostel. Each one has a different story. I know it seems strange that it's enough for me, but it is."

Wylie slipped her hand behind Amarina's neck. She stepped closer.

"As long as it's enough for you," she said.

"It is," Amarina practically whispered.

Wylie stared into Amarina's sea green eyes. She wanted to kiss her so desperately. Every muscle in her body was tensed as she waited for their lips to meet. But should she do it? She was still torn. She wondered if she should just have Amarina take her home. But, Lord, how she wanted her. So, what was the big deal?

She watched Amarina close her eyes and Wylie lost her battle with restraint. She lowered her lips and took Amarina's with her own. Her heart raced when their lips met. She wanted Amarina in the worst way.

She pulled away and waited until Amarina opened her eyes. She watched as they finally seemed to focus on her own.

"That was nice," Amarina said.

"Yes, it was."

"Your lips are so tender. Not what I'd expect from someone like you."

"Someone like me?"

"You know. Uberbutch."

"Oh. Got it. You know, you have very soft lips, as well."

"I do?"

"Yes. I enjoy kissing you," Wylie said.

"I don't know what it is about you," Amarina said. "You make me act differently than anybody else."

"How do you mean?"

"One minute I'm defensive, the next I'm inviting you back to my place. It's odd."

"Emotions are a funny thing," Wylie said.

Amarina backed away.

"I'm being a horrible hostess. Can I get you something to drink?"

Wylie took a calming breath.

"Um, sure. Have you got any beer?"

"I've got Red Ant. Is that okay?"

"I've no idea." Wylie laughed. "But I'm willing to try it."

"Great. I'll get one for each of us."

Amarina walked into the kitchen and Wylie leaned on the bar and watched her.

"I really love your place," she said. "I mean that. Such individuality."

"Thank you." Amarina handed her a beer and leaned on her side of the counter. "It suits me."

Wylie took a swig of the beer.

"This is really good," she said as she checked out the label. "How far is Adelaide from here?"

"It's at the Southern end of the country."

"Ah. So this isn't exactly a local beer."

"Not exactly."

"But still good."

"I'm glad you like it. It's my favorite beer."

Wylie stood where she was and wondered whether she should approach Amarina or whether she should wait for her to come around to her side of the bar. She reasoned she should wait. Tonight would be all about Amarina and her wants and needs. Wylie would force herself to be patient.

Amarina picked up her beer and walked back to the living room. She leaned back against the bar next to Wylie.

"Are you a big drinker?" Amarina said.

"I like my beer," Wylie said.

"But what about booze and such?"

"Not really. I mean, I've had several margaritas here, but that's because I'm on vacation, you know?"

"That's a good thing. I'm not much of a booze hound, either."

Wylie had to laugh. Amarina was so sweet looking. The idea of her being any kind of hound made Wylie chuckle.

"What?" Amarina said.

"You're just cute. I can't imagine you as a booze hound at all."

"Thanks. I think."

"You're a sweet person. I don't imagine you have too many vices."

Amarina turned so she was facing the same direction as Wylie.

"I really don't, I suppose."

"And that's a good thing."

"Good. I'm glad you don't think I'm too goody-goody."

"Not at all. I like you. Just the way you are."

Amarina didn't say anything, just stood there peeling the label off her beer bottle. Wylie opted not to point out the belief that such behavior meant one was sexually frustrated. She was surprised she hadn't peeled hers off herself. She was a bundle of hormones. She searched her mind for something to say. She really wanted to talk to Amarina. Sure, she wanted to have sex with her, but she also wanted to get to know her.

"So," she said, "before university, what was your favorite class? Like in high school or whatever you have here."

"Oh, that's easy. Arts and crafts. Any chance I had to take an art class, I did."

"Really? Are you any good? Or was it just for fun?"

"I did all the paintings in this room." Amarina turned around to face the living room again. Wylie did the same. She wandered around the small room and looked at the seascapes that hung on the walls.

"You're very talented," Wylie said.

"Thank you."

Wylie walked back to where Amarina stood. She took a long pull off her beer and leaned on the bar again, looking at Amarina. She ran her hands through her hair.

"You're very beautiful, you know."

"I'm just me."

"No. You're so much more than 'just' anything."

Amarina blushed and looked away.

"What?" Wylie said as she tilted Amarina's chin up and forced her to look at her.

"I don't know. You just always seem to know the right things to say."

"I tell the truth, Amarina. You're special. I knew that the first time I laid eyes on you."

"How could you have known?"

"You were one of the friendliest people I'd seen in a long time. I'd met nice people, don't get me wrong, but you were genuinely friendly. You read people and give them what they need. That's a special talent."

"I don't know that it's all that."

"You need to learn to take a compliment, young lady."

Amarina blushed deeper.

"How old are you?" Wylie asked.

"I'm twenty-five. How old are you?"

"Thirty-two."

"Do you think you're too old for me, then?" Amarina said.

"Not at all." Wylie closed the distance between them. "I think I'm the perfect age for you."

Amarina's head came to Wylie's neck, but Wylie didn't mind. She could bend over to kiss her. It didn't bother her at all. She leaned in slightly, but Amarina pulled away.

"Why don't we sit down?" she said.

"Sure," Wylie didn't let her frustration show. "Lead the way."

She followed Amarina across the room to the sofa and waited until she was seated. She sat next to her, close enough to feel the heat of her, but not quite touching her.

"You doin' okay?" Wylie said.

"Yeah. I think so."

"You scared?"

"Not scared so much as nervous."

"What can I do to help you with your nerves?" Wylie took her hand.

"That's nice," Amarina said.

"Yeah? Does that help?"

"A little."

Wylie stroked Amarina's thumb with her own. It did little to soothe her, but she hoped it calmed Amarina.

"You have the nicest touch," Amarina said.

"Thank you. Your hand is very soft."

"Yours is surprisingly soft, too. I mean, for the type of work you do."

"Yeah. I try not to let them get too rough."

"That must be hard."

"Nah. It just takes diligence."

Amarina turned their hands over and examined them.

"Your fingers are long."

"I'm quite a bit taller than you. It would make sense for my hands to be bigger than yours."

"True."

Amarina lifted their hands to her mouth and kissed the back of Wylie's. The kiss was soft and tentative and sent hot chills through Wylie's body.

"That was nice." Wylie tried to keep her voice steady. She kissed the back of Amarina's hand. "See?"

Amarina moved closer to Wylie. Wylie put her arm around her and pulled her to her.

"You doin' okay?"

"Yeah."

"Good." She kissed the top of her head, her temple, and then her cheek. She finally kissed her mouth again and this time it was harder, with more passion. Amarina responded in kind and Wylie's heart leapt in her chest. She thought she would burst with need. She pulled away, breathless.

Amarina sat there looking up at her. She wrapped her arms around Wylie's neck and pulled her to her again. Wylie ran her tongue along Amarina's lower lip until she opened her mouth and let Wylie in. They kissed like that for several minutes before Amarina broke the kiss.

"You okay?" Wylie asked.

Amarina nodded.

"Better than okay."

"Yeah?" Wylie smiled.

"Yeah." Amarina pulled Wylie to her again, lay back on the couch, and pulled Wylie on top of her. She opened her mouth and welcomed Wylie anew.

Wylie fought the urge to grind into Amarina. Instead, she kissed her passionately, but held herself up so their bodies didn't touch completely. It was no use. Amarina arched into her at the same time she pulled her down into her. Wylie was fighting a losing battle.

Wylie lowered herself into Amarina as the kissing intensified. Amarina spread her legs and Wylie brought her knee up to meet her.

Amarina tensed up and Wylie saw her eyes opened wide.

Wylie quickly moved her leg.

"No," Amarina said. "Bring it back. It just surprised me is all. It felt really good."

"Are you sure?"

"Positive."

Wylie went back to kissing her and moved her leg against her again. She could feel the moist warmth radiating from her and it was all she could do not to rip her dress off and have her. She kissed her harder and moved her hand down her back to cup her ass. Amarina responded by arching against her. Wylie felt the length of Amarina's body pressed into her and she once again cautioned herself to go slowly and take her time. She wanted this to be special.

She moved her mouth to kiss Amarina's neck and cheek. She whispered in her ear.

"You're driving me crazy."

"Me, too," Amarina said. "Kiss me again."

Wylie was happy to oblige. Kissing Amarina was like heaven on earth. She could go on doing it forever. She ground Amarina's pelvis into her own. The feeling almost made her come. The sensation sent shivers all over her body. When Amarina wrapped her legs around her, she almost lost it.

She managed to keep her composure, although every bit of her wanted to tear Amarina's dress off her and devour her. Amarina closed her ankles around Wylie's waist and tightened her grip around her neck. Wylie ground her pelvis into Amarina and she moaned into Wylie's mouth.

Wylie moved her hand back up Amarina's body and brought it around to cup a breast.

"I want to feel you," Amarina said. "Help me out of this dress."

Wylie hated to break the contact they already had, but longed to touch Amarina's skin. She climbed off her and stood on shaky legs. Amarina stood and leaned into Wylie.

"I'm a little dizzy," Amarina said.

"Nothing wrong with that."

Amarina turned so her back was to Wylie.

"Unzip my dress, please?"

Wylie did so quickly and efficiently. She pushed the shoulders off Amarina and guided the dress down her plump figure.

"You are so cute," Wylie said. "I love your body."

"I'm a little self-conscious about it."

"Don't be. You're beautiful. Now, can I take that bra off?"

Amarina blushed a deep red.

"If you're not ready, it's okay," Wylie said.

"No. Go ahead. Take it off."

Wylie deftly unhooked Amarina's bra and tossed it on the couch. She turned Amarina around to face her. Amarina looked up at her with what appeared to be fear in her eyes.

"Are you scared, baby?" Wylie said.

"I'll try not to be. I trust you."

"You know I don't expect this to be a one-time thing," Wylie said.

Amarina raised her eyebrows.

"You don't need to say that."

"I mean it, Amarina."

"I'd like that."

"Good," she said before she kissed her again.

Wylie moved her hands from Amarina's waist, up to cup her large breasts. She ran her thumbs over the nipples and coaxed them to attention. They were very responsive and Wylie was happy to see that. She was glad that Amarina was enjoying herself. She'd worried they might not get this far, but Amarina wasn't holding back. So far.

She sat on the couch and positioned Amarina between her legs. She leaned forward and took a nipple in her mouth while she kneaded the other breast.

"Oh my God. That feels so good," Amarina said.

Wylie sucked harder as she pulled Amarina's nipple against the roof of her mouth. She rolled her tongue over the tip of it as she sucked, which elicited a moan from Amarina. She leaned into Wylie and placed her hands on her shoulders to brace herself.

Wylie switched to the other nipple and felt Amarina shaking. She looked up at her.

"Are you okay?"

"My legs are shaking."

"Oh. I'm sorry." She scooted over. "Here. Sit down."

"Why don't we go to my room?" Amarina said.

CHAPTER TEN

Wylie stood and took Amarina's hand. Amarina led Wylie through some strings of sapphire beads into a small room. The queen-sized bed took up most of the room, but there was also a dresser and a dressing table. That was it. The bed was made and had a comforter that was dark blue with yellow moons and stars on it.

"I should have expected this," Wylie said.

Amarina smiled.

"I do have a style."

"That you do. And I like it."

"Thank you."

Wylie lay on the bed and patted the spot next to her.

"Shouldn't you take your clothes off, too?" Amarina asked.

"Sure."

Wylie stood and stripped. She watched closely as Amarina stepped out of her underwear. She was naked and beautiful and all hers. At least for the night. Wylie planned on it lasting more than just one night, but that ball was in Amarina's court now.

Wylie lay back down and reached her hand out. Amarina took it and lay down next to Wylie.

"You have the most amazing body," Wylie said.

"I'm pretty chunky."

"No. Your body is perfect. Don't let anyone tell you otherwise."

"I'm glad you like it."

"I love it."

Wylie went back to playing with Amarina's breasts. They were large, so large that one of them was too big for one of Wylie's hands. But Wylie wasn't complaining. She loved big breasts so she suckled, tugged, twisted, and tweaked Amarina's nipples. It didn't take long for her to realize just how sensitive Amarina was. She cried out several times while Wylie played.

"Wow," Wylie said. "So you like nipple play, huh?"

Amarina blushed a deep red.

"I really do."

"Well, that's good to know."

But it wasn't talking that Wylie wanted to do. She had so much more planned for Amarina. She kissed her again and moved her hand down her body to find where her legs met. She was extremely wet from the orgasms she'd already had.

"You feel so good," Wylie said. "You're so wet for me."

"You've got me so excited," Amarina said.

"Me, too, baby. Me, too."

"Yeah? Can I feel you?"

"Don't you want me to please you?" Wylie said.

"I just want to feel you first."

Wylie lay on her back and opened her legs. She felt Amarina's tentative touch and almost exploded.

"You're very wet, too," Amarina said.

"I'm very excited."

"I make you that way, huh?"

"Yes, you do."

"I like that," Amarina said as she dragged her hand between Wylie's legs.

Wylie reached down and grabbed Amarina's wrist.

"Okay, baby. It's my turn to please you. You can please me after."

"But you feel so good."

"I'll feel even better after I'm through loving you," Wylie said.

"Okay." She removed her hand.

Wylie rolled back to her side and placed her hand between Amarina's legs again. She lightly stroked her before tenderly entering her.

"That feels so good," Amarina said.

Wylie looked down at her and saw her eyes closed and close to a grimace on her face. She wondered if she was about to come again so soon. She moved her fingers in and out several times and Amarina screamed as she climaxed.

Wylie kissed her on her mouth, then kissed down her body. She stopped to kiss and suck each breast on her way. She finally positioned herself between her legs and took in all she saw.

"You're beautiful," she said.

Amarina didn't answer so Wylie stopped admiring and went to work. She had to taste Amarina's orgasms. There was no way she couldn't. She dragged her tongue all over her before licking her clit. She licked and flicked at it while she reached a hand up to play with a breast.

Amarina grabbed her hand and held it. She squeezed it hard when she cried out again as she came over and over. The extra connection made the orgasms that much sweeter for Wylie. She liked holding Amarina's hand.

She rested her face against Amarina's inner thigh and breathed in her scent. Her own clit was rock hard, but she wanted to admire Amarina just a little while longer.

"Come up here," Amarina finally said.

Wylie continued to hold Amarina's hand as she climbed up next to her. She liked the feel of it in hers. She lay next to her and pulled her close. She kissed her shoulder.

"You're easy to please. I like that."

"Is that really a good thing? Or are you just being nice?"

"How many times do I have to say that I'm an honest person, Amarina? I don't lie."

"Thank you, then."

"Oh, no. Thank *you*."

Amarina propped herself up on an elbow and looked up and down Wylie's body.

"You're so muscular," she said. "It makes me even more self-conscious."

"Don't be. I told you. I love your body."

Amarina let her hand cover the length of Wylie's body before coming back to touch a breast.

Her touch was so soft, so tender that Wylie didn't know how long she'd be able to hold out.

"I don't have as much experience as you," Amarina said.

"What makes you think I have experience?"

"I can tell."

"Fair enough. Have you ever been with a woman before?"

"Oh, sure. But it's been a while."

"I'm in no hurry. Take your time. Explore. Find your groove."

"Really? You're okay if I'm a little rusty?"

"I'm fine with that. The way you touch me makes me crazy. I don't mind if it takes a little while. I'll enjoy the process. I promise."

Amarina moved her hand to where Wylie had spread her legs for her. Her fingers touched Wylie lightly, everywhere from her clit down. Wylie closed her eyes and reveled in the feeling. Somehow the uncertainty of Amarina's touch added to Wylie's arousal.

"I want to see you," Amarina said. She moved down the bed until she was between Wylie's legs. "I see what you meant. You're beautiful too."

She stroked Wylie's hard clit. Wylie ground her teeth to keep from coming too soon. She wanted Amarina to enjoy herself, even though it was driving her wild.

"Your clit is so big," Amarina said. "And it's so slick."

She lowered her head and ran her tongue over it.

"Oh, God," Wylie moaned.

"Are you okay?" Amarina asked.

"I'm fine. Please. Don't stop."

Amarina paused before going back to licking Wylie. She ran her fingers along her again, this time plunging them inside. Wylie arched her back to take her in as deep as she could. Amarina licked Wylie's clit again and Wylie could take no more. She cried out as the waves of orgasms washed over her.

When her head had quit spinning, she tapped Amarina on her head.

"Hey, you. Come on up here."

"I'm so happy I made you come," Amarina said when she was lying next to Wylie.

"Me, too." Wylie laughed.

"I want to do it again."

"You will. Many times, if I have my way."

"Really?"

"Yep. I really like you, Amarina."

"I really like you, too, Wylie."

They drifted off to sleep in each other's arms.

Wylie awoke the next morning to Amarina between her legs again. She was already teetering on the brink of an orgasm by the time she was fully conscious.

"Good morning," she said hoarsely.

She got no response as Amarina's mouth was full. Wylie didn't fight it, she let herself go, and the climax hit her hard. She reached out her arm and Amarina moved next to her.

"What brought that on?" Wylie said.

"I told you last night I wanted to do it again. So I did."

"And now it's your turn."

"Nope." Amarina climbed out of bed. "We need to get a move on. We have to meet my brother soon."

"Okay. Do we have time for me to treat you to breakfast?"

"Sure. I'll just take a quick shower."

"I'll join you."

"No offense, but I don't think I trust you in the same shower with me. Like I said, not today. Some other time for sure."

"Fine. I'll wait my turn." She sat on the bed and smiled. Amarina had spunk, she had to hand it to her. And she wasn't going to let Wylie just have her way with her. Wylie was definitely going to have her hands full with this one. And she was a-okay with that.

When it was her turn to shower, Wylie did so quickly as she was excited to start their day together. She got out of the shower with her towel wrapped around her waist and went in the bedroom to get her clothes. She found Amarina sitting on the bed.

"What are you doing?" she asked.

"Um, I don't, I don't," Amarina stammered, "I was waiting for you. I guess I didn't think it through."

"It's okay by me. You saw more of me last night."

"No," Amarina said and left the room.

Wylie had to chuckle. Amarina was so naïve sometimes. She was such an innocent and Wylie really liked that about her. She was used to much more experienced, worldly women, but Amarina was a welcome change from all that. She dressed quickly and went out to the kitchen.

"Do I smell coffee?" she said.

"Yes, you do. What do you take with it?"

"I take it black."

She took the cup of coffee from Amarina and took a tentative sip. She'd learned that Australians liked their coffee strong.

"This is good," she said.

"I'm glad you like it. Drink up. We need to head out in a few."

Wylie finished her coffee and put the cup in the sink.

"Do we have time to swing by the hostel so I can put on some clean clothes?"

"Sure. Let's go."

They drove to the hostel and Wylie went to her room while Amarina went into the office. Wylie changed and brushed her teeth, then headed back to the lobby to meet up with Amarina.

"Everything okay here?" she asked.

"Yep. I just thought I'd check in since I was here."

Amarina drove them to a small café in the center of town where they had croissants and coffee.

"How are you doing this morning? Really?" Wylie asked.

"I'm fine."

"Fine? That's all? Don't you want to talk about it?"

"Not here. Not now. Come on. We need to get going."

"Fair enough. Now, where do we meet your brother?"

"At a small airstrip at the edge of town."

The airstrip was tiny. It was for private planes only. They met Amarina's brother James in the office.

"I've got all my paperwork filed," he said. "We're ready to take off."

They crossed the tarmac to his little plane. Wylie's stomach was all over the place, she was so excited. She climbed in the back with Amarina, strapped in and reached for Amarina's hand. Amarina pulled her hand away and shook her head.

"Are you scared?" Amarina asked.

"No. Just excited."

"Good."

James took off and Wylie sat back and gazed out the window as she knew the wonders of nature would soon appear below her. She was right. At first, he flew out over the ocean and Wylie got to see all the wild rock formations that bordered one area of the water. He flew them up to where the beach was gone, with sheer rock walls taking its place. He then turned inland and they flew over the red dirt that Wylie had become accustomed to. The contrast of the red dirt with the crystal blue water of the river took her breath away.

He flew low over the gorges and she was able to see kangaroos and wallabies below them. It was a wonderful way to spend the day. She looked over at Amarina and Amarina smiled at her. Life was good.

When James finally landed the plane, it was late afternoon and Wylie was starved.

"Would you like to join us for dinner?" she asked James.

He seemed to consider it for a moment, then looked at Amarina then back to Wylie.

"No, thanks. You two go on."

"But I'd like to thank you for the sight-seeing trip."

"It was my pleasure, believe me. And I've got plans this evening. Maybe some other time?"

"Sounds good."

They left the airport, and Amarina looked over at Wylie.

"That was nice of you to invite James to dinner."

"It was the least I could do."

"It felt good to hear we're going to have dinner again tonight," Amarina said.

"Oh yeah. I suppose I should have asked."

"It's okay," Amarina laughed. "I don't mind spending more time with you. Will you be spending the night with me again?"

"I'd like that very much."

"Good. Me, too."

"So, how about an early dinner?" Wylie said.

"Sure thing. It's my turn to choose a restaurant, though."

"Fair enough."

She drove through town and stopped at a small out of the way place.

"How does something located this far off the shore front stay in business?" Wylie asked.

"It's really popular with locals."

"Ah. Then it must be good."

"Very."

"So, what's good?" Wylie said when they were seated.

"Do you trust me to order for you?"

"Sure." Wylie set her menu down and leaned back in the booth. She looked around the small place. It had a large tuna hanging on one wall and paintings of the general Broome area hanging on the others. It was a quaint little place and it smelled amazing. The wafting odors from the kitchen had her stomach growling and her mouth watering.

The waiter came over and Amarina ordered for them. Wylie had to smile. She was such a contradiction. One minute, she was shy and insecure and the next minute she was ordering dinner for both of them. That was okay, though. Wylie liked both sides.

"So, what did you order me?" Wylie said.

"Barramundi with cuttlefish. I hope you like fish."

"I do. Very much. I'm excited to try this."

They talked about their day as they ate their dinner, then Amarina grew quiet after the waiter had taken their plates.

"You okay?" Wylie asked.

"Yeah. Just nervous."

"Would you rather just take me home?"

"No. I know what I want. I'm just nervous about it."

"Well, last night was fun, right?" Wylie said.

"Yes."

"So, tonight will be just like that."

"I hope so. I'm just afraid I'll disappoint you."

"Baby, you couldn't."

"I like it when you call me baby."

"Good. I'll do it more often."

The check came and Wylie paid it then they walked out to Amarina's car. Wylie leaned Amarina into her car door and looked deeply into her eyes.

"I don't know what to say to you, Amarina. You stir something in me I've never felt before."

"That makes me feel good."

Wylie brushed an imaginary strand of hair off Amarina's face.

"Can I kiss you?"

"I wish you would."

Wylie lowered her mouth and claimed Amarina's. It was a powerful kiss, full of the promise of what would happen when they got home.

"Let's get out of here," she said when the kiss finally ended.

They drove home in silence, with Wylie aware of nothing but the throbbing between her legs.

"Would you like a beer?" Amarina said.

"Sure. I'll take one."

Amarina returned with two beers and they sat together on the couch.

"You know, just being close to you makes me crazy," Wylie said.

"Me, too."

"Yeah?"

"Yeah."

Wylie kissed Amarina then. A long, slow kiss that ended with Amarina opening her mouth and allowing Wylie in. Wylie moved her tongue all over the inside of Amarina's mouth, playing with her tongue and exploring every inch. She was breathless when the kiss ended.

She took a long pull on her beer and tried to cool the fire that was raging inside her.

"I love the way you kiss me," Amarina said.

"I love kissing you."

Wylie took Amarina's beer and placed them both on the coffee table. She leaned Amarina back on the couch and climbed on top of her. She kissed her mouth, her cheek and her neck. She nibbled on her earlobe then kissed her mouth again. She was a torrent of hormones and had to have Amarina, and soon.

She reached her hand down and unbuttoned Amarina's shorts. She fumbled with the zipper, but soon had it down. She slid her hand under Amarina's blouse and cupped one of her full breasts.

She needed more. She told herself to slow down, but it wasn't easy.

"God I need you," she whispered in Amarina's ear.

Amarina spread her legs and Wylie reached between them and teased her through her underwear.

"Let me take them off," Amarina said.

"Not yet." Wylie was shaking with her need to please Amarina, but she wanted to tease her just a little. Not much, because she knew she wouldn't last that long. "Do you want to go to your room?"

"No. I don't want to wait that long."

Wylie smiled. She didn't want to wait that long either.

Amarina decided to take it upon herself to get naked. She wriggled out of her shorts and panties and lay naked from the waist down for Wylie's pleasure. Wylie's fingers were inside her immediately. She was soft and wet and Wylie couldn't resist.

"Oh, baby," she murmured. "You feel so good."

She thrust deep inside Amarina and Amarina met each one. Wylie was so excited, she thought she might come before Amarina. But it took no time for Amarina to scream her name.

Wylie lay on top of Amarina, both of them breathing heavily.

"You're amazing," Wylie said. "You're so easy to please. I love it."

"I love how you make me feel."

"I want to make you feel that way again and again."

CHAPTER ELEVEN

Wylie struggled to get Amarina's shirt off.

"Sit up," she said.

Amarina sat up straight and removed her shirt. She took her bra off then lay back down on the couch.

"I love your breasts," Wylie said. She took them lovingly in her hands and squeezed them. She took a nipple in her mouth and played over it with her tongue. She felt Amarina's fingernails dig into her back as she came.

Wylie moved to the other nipple and sucked and licked it while she pinched the first. Again, in no time, Amarina was crying out her name.

Wylie still hadn't had enough. She moved her hand between Amarina's legs again. She stroked her slick clit until she came again for her.

"I can't take anymore," Amarina said.

"Sure you can."

"No. I can't. We need to get you naked so I can play with you."

The idea sounded wonderful to Wylie, who was a wet, throbbing mess.

"Shall we go to your bedroom?"

"Yes."

Amarina gathered her clothes off the floor and did her best to cover herself with them.

"You know I mean it when I say I love your body," Wylie said. "You shouldn't cover it up."

"I'm self-conscious. I told you."

"Okay, but I wish you wouldn't be. I want to see all your curves all the time."

"I'll work on it."

Wylie reached out her hand.

"Here. Hand them to me."

Amarina stood silently and shifted from one foot to the other.

"Come on, baby. Let me have the clothes."

Amarina slowly handed them to Wylie, who placed them on the couch and admired Amarina.

"You're simply gorgeous," she said. "Don't let anybody ever tell you otherwise."

Amarina couldn't even meet her eyes. Wylie placed her hand lightly on her chin and lifted her face.

"I mean it," she said.

"Okay."

"Now let's get into that bedroom. I'm going to burst on my own if you don't touch me soon."

Wylie stripped out of her clothes and lay on the bed. Amarina stood over her and stared down at her.

"Open your legs," she said.

Wylie did as she was instructed. The feel of Amarina's gaze on her made her clit grow.

"I like to look at you," Amarina said.

"I like it when you look at me."

Amarina settled herself between Wylie's legs. She dragged her hand along her then lowered her mouth to lick her.

Wylie grabbed the sheets. Amarina drove her crazy. Sure, she wasn't as experienced as some of the women Wylie had been with, but that just made her more attractive and turned her on more.

"Jesus, what you do to me," she groaned.

Amarina looked up from what she was doing.

"I make you feel good?"

"Dear God, yes."

Amarina lowered her mouth again and got back to pleasing Wylie. Her uncertainty still evident, she seemed to gain confidence as she went and soon Wylie felt the energy forming in her center. She tried to hold off and enjoy as long as she could but it was no use. She came hard and fast several times.

"I'm so glad you like what I do to you," Amarina said.

"The question is, do *you* like what you do?"

"What do you mean?"

"I mean is it enjoyable for you to have your hands and mouth on me."

"Oh, heck yeah."

"Good. I'd hate for it to be a chore."

"Not at all," Amarina said. "Not even close. I could stay here forever."

Wylie laughed.

"I'm glad to hear that. But why don't you come on up here and let me hold you."

Amarina climbed next to Wylie.

"So, what time do you have to be at work tomorrow?" Wylie asked.

"I should be there by eight."

"Oh wow. Early morning for us, then, huh?"

"I suppose. I'm an early riser anyway."

"So am I, honestly. I sure hope I hear from that pearl place soon."

"Did you really apply for a job here?" Amarina said.

"I did. I'd like to stay here a while longer."

"I'd like that, too."

"I'd really like to keep seeing you, Amarina."

"Me, too. I really like you. How long do you think you'll stay around for?"

"I'm not sure, baby. Hopefully quite a while."

"That would be wonderful."

They fell asleep in each other's arms and woke with Amarina's alarm.

"Do I get to shower with you this morning?" Wylie asked.

"Do you really want to?"

"I do."

"Come on then. And don't make me late."

"I'll try not to."

They got in the shower and Wylie couldn't resist Amarina's body. Just as she'd known she wouldn't be able to. The water cascaded down Amarina's curves and dripped to the floor. Wylie bent to lick water off her breasts. Amarina's nipples hardened at the contact.

She pressed Amarina back against the wall and bent to her knees. She buried her face between Amarina's legs and lapped greedily at her. She eased up and made lazy circles around her clit. She felt Amarina's legs start to shake, so she finished her off with one sweep of her tongue.

"Oh, my God. You're so dangerous," Amarina said.

"In a good way, I hope," Wylie said when she was standing again.

"In a very good way. Now hurry up and get clean. I need to get to work."

They arrived at the hostel just before eight.

"You have a few minutes. Come to my room with me," Wylie said.

"Why?"

"So I can kiss you good-bye properly."

Amarina blushed. She was so damned cute, Wylie thought.

"Okay. But just for a moment."

"I know."

They walked hand in hand back to Wylie's room and as soon as she closed the door, she took Amarina in her arms.

"I wish you didn't have to work today."

"Me, too. What are you going to do all day?"

"Probably hit the beach. Maybe go fishing. We'll see."

"Okay. Well, have fun. Now kiss me good-bye. I need to get to the office."

Wylie pressed her mouth to Amarina's and ran her tongue along her lips. Amarina opened her mouth and their tongues danced together briefly. Amarina ended the kiss and looked hard at Wylie.

"Will I see you tonight?" she asked.

"I certainly hope so. Can I take you to dinner again?"

"That would be wonderful."

"What time should I be here?"

"Five."

"Okay, baby. I'll see you then."

She watched Amarina walk down the sidewalk and turn into the office, already craving her body again.

Wylie switched into her board shorts and T-shirt and headed for the water. She was looking forward to a day lounging around. She was walking along the beach when her phone rang.

"Hello?" she said.

"Wylie Boase, please," the voice on the other line said.

"This is."

"This is Ronald. I'm calling from Turquoise Sea Pearls. I'd like you to come in for an interview."

"Great. When?"

"Can you come in at eleven?"

"Today?"

"Yes."

"Yes, sir. I'll be there."

"Great. We'll see you then."

"Good-bye."

"Good-bye."

Wylie's stomach was in her throat. She was so excited. If she got this job, she could stay for who knew how long? She turned around and went back to her room. She made a pit stop in the lobby.

"What are you doing here?" Amarina asked.

"I'm actually checking to see if there might be an iron here I can borrow."

"Yes. We have one. But, you know, I have one at home. You could have used it."

"I didn't know I had a job interview then."

"A job interview? That's fantastic," Amarina said.

"Yeah. I just need to iron some clothes so I'll look presentable."

Amarina went into a little closet and came out with an ironing board and iron.

"Here you go. Just be sure to return them when you're through."

"If it means another chance to see you, you know I will."

She took them and went to her room. She ironed a pair of long khaki pants and a Kelly green golf shirt. She dressed and took the ironing board and iron back to the lobby.

"Wow," Amarina said. "You look amazing."

"Thanks. I'm hot as hell, though." She laughed.

"You are hot," Amarina said.

"Thank you. Well, here's your stuff back."

"Thanks for bringing them back. You never know when someone might need them."

"No worries."

"What time's your interview?"

"It's at eleven. I'm gonna go get a bite to eat then head over."

"Well, good luck."

"Thanks."

Wylie arrived at the office at five minutes before eleven. Nadine was at the desk. Wylie approached her.

"I'm Wylie Boase. I have an eleven o'clock with Ronald."

"Of course. Please. Sit down and I'll let him know you're here."

Ronald came out to get her. He was a tall man, who stood about six foot four. He was solid muscle, though. She didn't think he had an ounce of fat on him. She stood to her full five ten and shook his hand firmly.

"Come on in, Wylie."

He showed her to his office. It was small, with pictures of pearl divers and fishermen on the wall. He noticed her looking at them.

"These are some of our employees over the years. We have fun."

"It looks like it."

"So, Wylie. I'll be honest. You look great on paper. Tell me why you think you'd be a good pearl diver."

"Well, sir..."

"No 'sir' here. I'm Ronald."

"Yes, sir, er, Ronald. I'm used to manual labor. I'm a bricklayer. So I'm used to working hard. I'm not afraid to get dirty if that's what it takes. And I have my PADI certification, so this wouldn't be the first time I've done underwater diving."

"These are all good things. We work on a farm, so there's more to it than simply diving for pearls. But you sound like you can handle it. And, of course, if we get out there and you can't, we part ways."

"Understandable."

"When can you start?"

"When do you need me?"

"Say Monday?"

"That will be great. I'll be here. What time?"

"Don't be here. Meet us at the dock. Boat leaves at six. Don't be late."

He stood and she stood and shook his hand again. He gave her a map showing her where the dock was and she walked out into the hot sun, all smiles.

She stopped by the lobby to tell Amarina the good news.

"That's great!" Amarina said. "How long will you be working for him?"

"I guess until I quit. Or get fired. And I don't think that's going to happen."

"That's really great news, Wylie."

"Yeah. I couldn't wait to tell you. Okay. I've got to get out of these clothes and get in the water. I'll see you around five."

"I'll be waiting."

Wylie felt refreshed and energized when she got back from the beach. She stopped by the lobby to see Amarina.

"Hey there," she said.

"Hey yourself. How was your day?"

"Amazing. The water always does something for me. How was your day?"

"Mellow."

"That's a good thing, right?"

"Oh, yes."

"Right on. Well, let me go get showered and I'll be right back."

"Sounds good to me. I'm ready to get out of here for the night."

Wylie cleaned away the sand and saltwater and felt fresh as she dressed to go meet Amarina. She went to the lobby and found her with a long face.

"What's up?"

"My replacement is running late," Amarina said. "I can't leave for a while yet."

"That sucks."

"Yeah. Sorry about that."

"No worries. Can I just hang out here with you?"

"You could, but it would be mighty boring. Plus I have some office stuff I could take care of while I wait."

"Okay then. I'll go hang out by the pool. Come get me when you're ready."

"Okay."

Wylie wandered out to the pool. There were several people out there. One woman in particular caught her eye. She was a buxom brunette who carried herself like she knew how to get what she wanted. She strolled right over to Wylie and sat next to her. Wylie made a point not to look at the woman, whose breasts were barely contained by her suit.

"Are you new here?" the woman asked.

"That depends on your definition of new. I've been here about a week."

"How come I've never seen you here before? And where's your suit?"

"I'm actually meeting someone for dinner."

At that moment, Amarina stepped into the pool area. Wylie rose with a sigh of relief and walked over to meet her.

"Looks like Susan took an interest in you," Amarina said.

"Is that her name? We didn't get that far."

"Good."

"Are you jealous?" Wylie teased her.

"I don't know. After Kathryn, I guess I'm not quite sure what to expect."

"Hey, baby. Kathryn was someone to pass a few nights with. You're different."

"But Susan is gorgeous."

"I'm into *you*, Amarina. Not Susan. Not anyone else. Just you."

"Are you sure?"

"Positive." She took Amarina's hand. It was soft and warm and she gave it a slight squeeze.

They walked out to Amarina's car.

"So it didn't embarrass you to be seen with me? I mean, with Susan talking to you then me walking up?"

"No, baby. You're beautiful. I don't know why you don't see that. I'm proud to be seen with you."

They drove to an oceanfront restaurant and got a table on the patio.

"You know, I think you're crazy for always wanting to sit outside. It's bloody hot out here."

"It's not that bad," Wylie said.

"I prefer air conditioning."

"Okay, then, let's go inside."

"No. We can see the water from here. And you're right. It's really not that bad."

"Are you sure?" Wylie said.

"I'm sure."

They ate their dinner and watched the sunset. Afterward, they went for a moonlit walk along the beach. They had to move out of the way of some camels, but outside of that group, they had the beach to themselves.

They sat and talked for a while. Wylie draped her arm over Amarina's shoulders while they talked about their days.

"Shall we head back to your place?" Wylie said.

"Sure."

They stood up and dusted the sand off.

"I'd hate to get sand in your car," Wylie said. "Maybe sitting out here wasn't such a good idea."

"Are you kidding? My car's a heap. I don't care about sand in it."

"Your car's fine."

"It's a heap. And I don't mind. She gets me from place to place. I don't need anything else."

"I love your attitude," Wylie said. "Usually, anyway."

"Usually?"

"I don't like your attitude toward yourself, baby. I wish you could see what I see."

"I'll try."

"Thank you."

Chapter Twelve

They got back to Amarina's place.

"I'm getting used to being here," Wylie said.

"You are? Is that a good thing?"

"Sure. Why not?"

"I don't know. I don't want you to think about moving in or anything."

Wylie laughed.

"Baby, we've gone on a couple of dates. I'm totally into you, but it's way too soon to be thinking like that."

"Good. Just so we're both clear."

"We are."

Wylie was thinking how refreshing it was to have someone on the same page she was. She liked dating, okay, sleeping with women, but she wasn't much into commitment. Amarina was different for sure. Wylie was perfectly comfortable making a commitment to her. Odd, but true. She still wasn't ready to move in, though, and she was glad Amarina felt the same way.

"I'll grab us each a beer," Amarina said and Wylie made herself at home on the couch. She slipped off her sandals and put her feet on the coffee table. It might have been considered rude, but she'd seen Amarina do it, so figured it must be okay.

Amarina returned with the beer. She handed one to Wylie then knelt next to her.

"You don't look comfortable," Wylie said.

"I'm fine. I want you, though. I figure this way I can assault you easily."

"Assault me, huh?" Wylie laughed.

"Yep." Amarina was laughing, too. She made her way close to Wylie and kissed her neck.

"You're going to spill your beer," Wylie said.

"No, I won't." She kissed her neck again and lightly sucked on it.

Wylie grew dizzy at the sensation. Amarina's shyness seemed to be on holiday and Wylie liked it. A lot.

Amarina sat down and drank some beer.

"You sure know how to get me going," Wylie said.

"And then I stopped. Does that make me a tease?"

"No. Because I know what's coming later."

"So do I." Amarina smiled.

"But for future reference, anytime you want to suck on my neck, you feel free to do so."

"Good to know."

Wylie sat sipping her beer. She had something she wanted to say but wasn't sure how to go about it. Finally, she set her beer down and turned to face Amarina.

"There's something I want to tell you, Amarina."

"Uh-oh. This can't be good."

"Oh no. It's good. At least I think it's good."

"If it's good, why am I scared?"

"I just want you to know…I mean, I think it's important for me to tell you…"

"What? You have an STD or something? What is it? Spit it out."

"No, no, no. Nothing like that. It's just that I really like you."

"I like you, too," Amarina said. "I thought we'd established that already."

"We have. I mean…what I'm trying to say is it's more than just sex for me. And I want you to know that."

"Really?"

"Really. And I think it's important that you know that."

"I feel the same way, so it's a relief to hear that."

"Yeah?"

"Yeah."

"Good." Wylie let out her breath and sat back against the couch. She reached for her beer. "I'm glad we had that talk. I really want you to know you're different for me."

"Well, I've never been the type to sleep around, so I can't say you're different for me like that. But you feel different. I don't know."

"Good. I hope this is different for both of us."

She took Amarina's hand and they sat quietly for a few minutes.

"So, should we not have sex all the time then?" Amarina asked.

"What? Why not?"

"Just to be sure. I don't know," Amarina said again.

"I know I'm sure. And loving you is one way for me to prove myself to you. I wouldn't mind if you just wanted me to hold you sometimes, but I don't see anything wrong with making love every night."

"Okay. I was just checking."

"Don't you enjoy making love?" Wylie said.

"Of course I do. You make me feel things I've never felt before."

"Excellent. So, um, why don't we take this conversation into the bedroom?"

"Sounds good to me."

They made love for hours that night, until Amarina had to beg Wylie to stop, claiming she had to be at work in the morning.

Wylie spent the next few days at the beach, passing the time until Amarina got off work. Then, they'd go out to dinner then back to Amarina's place where they'd make love until late at night.

Sunday was Amarina's day off again. They lay in bed until eight, then got up and dressed and packed supplies for a day's hike in the gorge. Amarina did a great job keeping up with Wylie who had much longer legs and therefore strides.

They swam in the river and dried out by the trail. It was a beautiful day. One Wylie hated to see come to an end. They went back to Amarina's, where Wylie grilled some tuna for them while Amarina made a salad.

"I'm wondering if I should sleep at my own place," Wylie said at dinner.

"Why?"

"I have to be there by six. I'll need to change and stuff first."

"Well, we could both stay at your place."

"Are you sure?"

"Yes, I'm sure," Amarina said. "We'll finish dinner, do the dishes, then head over to your place."

"But my room is small and my bed isn't as big as yours. Not even close."

"I know that. I know how small the rooms are in my own hostel, Wylie." She laughed.

"Oh yeah. I suppose you would."

They finished their dinners and did the dishes together. They drove to the hostel and Amarina parked in her usual spot.

"People are going to talk," Wylie said.

"Do you think? I don't know. Maybe they'll just think I left my car here overnight. As long as they don't know about you, it'll be okay."

They walked back to Wylie's room, and she still fought the embarrassment at how tiny it was. Of course Amarina knew where she lived, but she'd never brought her back there. She was as nervous as a schoolgirl.

She was thankful she kept things as tidy as she did when she opened the door to let Amarina walk in.

"That bed is small," Amarina said.

"We'll both fit, though."

"I'm sure we will."

Wylie was keyed up, anxious to start her new job the next morning. She didn't know if she'd be able to sleep.

"You okay?" Amarina stepped toward her.

"Yeah. Just amped for tomorrow."

Amarina tugged at the bottom of Wylie's shirt.

"I think I know what may take your mind off it." She lifted the shirt over Wylie's head.

"I like the way you think."

She took her undershirt off and stood there while Amarina explored her upper body with her hands and mouth. She stood as long as her legs would hold her.

"We need to move to the bed," she said.

"Okay."

Amarina stripped as Wylie removed the rest of her clothes. They lay together on the bed with Amarina on top. She went back to worshipping Wylie's breasts before she kissed her way down her body. She ended up between her legs.

"This is my favorite place in the world," Amarina said.

"I like it when you're there, too."

Amarina licked and sucked Wylie until Wylie could take no more. She held her breath, then exhaled mightily as she climaxed. Amarina didn't stop, though.

"Hey. That's enough," Wylie said.

"No. I want you exhausted enough to sleep."

"But I want to take care of you now."

"Nope. Tonight is all about you."

Wylie laid back and let Amarina do her thing. She took her to orgasm after orgasm until Wylie was thoroughly spent.

"Come here, you," Wylie said. "Come snuggle with me."

Amarina did and Wylie held her as they both fell asleep.

Morning came very early. Wylie realized sleepily that Amarina wasn't in bed with her. She sat up and was relieved to see her across the room making coffee.

"You got up earlier than I did," Wylie said.

"My internal alarm is really good. And I knew you had to get up soon. Coffee should be done in a little while. Why don't you get ready for work?"

The sun was just coming up as Wylie put on her board shorts and T-shirt. She grabbed her SCUBA gear and wetsuit and put it in a small duffel bag. She was ready to go. She gladly accepted the cup of coffee Amarina offered her.

"You need to learn which coffee to buy, for future reference," Amarina said. "This stuff is shite."

"Sorry about that. It has caffeine, though, and that's what I need right now. Thanks for brewing it."

"My pleasure. Now, do you want a ride to the dock?"

"That would be great."

They got there at quarter of six. There were already some people waiting around.

"Well, this is it," Wylie said.

"Are you nervous?"

"I am. I don't know why."

"You'll have fun."

"I sure hope so."

They kissed good-bye and Wylie got out of the car. She walked over to the small group on the dock.

"Is this where I need to be for Turquoise Sea Pearls?"

"Yep," one woman said. "We call it TSP for short."

"Thanks. Otherwise it's a mouthful," Wylie said. "How long have you worked here?"

"Three years. The rest of these guys are new, just like you."

Wylie waved at the rest of the people on the dock.

"What's in the duffel bag?" the woman asked.

"My SCUBA gear."

"You won't need that. You'll need a wetsuit, but not the tanks."

"Seriously?" Wylie said.

"Yep. You breathe through a line that's attached to the drift boat. You'll learn all about it today."

Soon many more people were milling about on the dock. Wylie was getting more and more nervous. Or excited. She couldn't tell which. The idea of not wearing her SCUBA gear had her more than a little disconcerted. Still, she was excited to try this new line of work.

The boat arrived and they all got on it. Wylie stuck close to the woman from the dock until the newbies were called aside by a man. He spoke to them as the boat headed out.

"My name is Tink. I'll be in charge of you all today. One thing you'll need to know is how this boat operates," he told them. He took them on a tour of the vessel and showed them which gauges meant what and what knobs controlled what.

Wylie's head was spinning. She thought she had a grasp of it, but couldn't be sure.

"I don't expect you to remember all of this today," Tink said. "We'll go over it every day this week. You'll be tested Friday. We're not joking when we say it's important you know your stuff."

The boat anchored finally and several smaller boats were lowered into the water.

"These are booms," Tink said. "These are the boats that you will be attached to while drift diving. Now, for the next few days, you won't actually be picking up shells. You're just going to get used to drifting. That means holding on to the weighted work line and keeping your mouth on the long air hoses. That's what's keeping you attached to the boat. You do this for twenty minutes a pop, then thirty minutes. Tomorrow we'll work up to forty. Then, in a few days, you'll do that and pick up shells. For training, you'll have an expert diver with you. Now, go get your wetsuits on and get back here."

Wylie realized she had signed up for very hard work. Though the money promised to be good and would allow her to stay in Broome a little while longer. She hurried into her wetsuit and went back to join the others.

The woman from the dock was at her side.

"I'm Laurie," she said. "I'll be beside you on your dives today. Do you think you can handle things?"

"I think so."

"Good. If you get into trouble, let me know."

"Will do."

Laurie and Wylie went with four other people on one boom. It looked like a trawler to Wylie. She gathered with the others around the captain.

"You're each paired up with a master diver," she said. "Use him or her. If you're in trouble, let them know. It's imperative we find out if you can do this. If not, we need to part ways. For both our benefits. Now your first dive will only be twenty minutes. Put the breather end of the hose in your mouth. Climb in the water holding on to the weighted line. Drop down it until you reach the bottom. Hold on for twenty minutes and we'll bring you up. Understood?"

They all nodded. It sounded easy enough to Wylie.

"You go first," Laurie said. "I'll be right behind you."

Wylie put the hose in her mouth and grabbed hold of the line. She jumped in the water and followed the weighted line to the bottom. Sure enough, Laurie was right next to her. When everyone was in place, the boat started. It didn't go very fast, so Wylie had no trouble holding on.

The gist of it was easy. It got a little monotonous to hear nothing but the whirl of the propeller, but she held on and was actually surprised when Laurie motioned it was time to climb up.

They sat on the deck.

"We normally get twenty minutes on deck between dives," Laurie said. "It's time you use to clean your shells and catch your breath."

The day progressed with more dives. Wylie had no problem with any of them. One of the newbies did, though. They had to pull him up during one of the thirty-minute dives. She didn't see what happened, just saw him being helped up out of the water out of her peripheral vision.

The boom took them back to the main vessel where they all climbed in and changed out of their wetsuits.

"You did good today," Laurie said.

"Thanks. I'm glad you were there for me, just in case."

"I don't think you're going to have any trouble. It's not easy to be holding on with one hand and scooping shells with the other. It takes some getting used to, but so far, you seem to be a natural."

"I hope so. I really want to do this."

The boat took them back to the dock.

"We're heading out for beers," Laurie said. "Care to join us?"

Wylie checked her watch. She had a half hour before Amarina would be off work.

"Sure."

They walked over to a waterfront dive and Wylie had one beer before getting up to leave.

"What's the hurry?" Laurie asked. "You earned more than just one beer today."

"I've got to meet someone at five."

"Ah. I see. Bummer. Maybe tomorrow?"

"Yeah. Maybe."

She withdrew some cash from her wallet.

"No way," Laurie said. "This one's on me."

"Thank you," Wylie said.

"No problem. Now you'd better get going."

"I'm out of here. See you in the morning."

She hiked down the street and got to the hostel at about five fifteen. Amarina was sitting behind a desk in the office.

"Hey. Sorry I'm late. I went out for a beer with the gang," Wylie said.

"Oh, good. And you're not that late. How was your first day of work?"

"Easy," Wylie said. "Not like piece of cake easy, but pretty easy."

"Right on. I was worried. I've heard horror stories, you know."

"Yeah. We've all heard them. They had to pull one guy up today. I don't know what happened, but I guess he won't be back."

"So, how many oysters did you get?" Amarina said.

"None. We were just training today. I don't get to get oysters for a few days."

"Okay. That makes sense. And it makes me happy. I'd rather see you fully trained."

"Me, too. Now, how about dinner? I'm famished."

"Did you want to put some clothes on?" Amarina said.

"Oh yeah. I should. Come with me to my room?"

They walked back to her room where Amarina waited while she quickly showered and put on clean clothes.

"Do you want to take some things to my house?" Amarina said. "You can use my washer and dryer instead of the public one here. And we can sleep there where there's more room."

"That sounds great," Wylie said. She stuffed a bunch of clothes into a laundry bag and threw in her wet shorts and shirt and followed Amarina out to the car.

"What are you in the mood for for dinner?" Amarina said.

"I want a big ol' steak and some prawns. How does that sound?"

"Expensive, but delicious."

"I'm making good money now, baby. Let's do it."

CHAPTER THIRTEEN

After dinner, they drove back to Amarina's place. Wylie started a load of laundry, then grabbed two beers and joined Amarina on the couch.

"Man, am I beat," she said.

"Too beat?" Amarina sidled close.

"Never."

"So, tell me about your new workmates."

"I don't know many of them. I was teamed up with a woman named Laurie. She's showing me the ropes and making sure I'm safe."

"Laurie, huh?"

"Yeah. She's really nice. And knows her stuff. Hey, why don't you join us for beers tomorrow after work? You could meet her and the others."

"That sounds like a good idea. Otherwise I might get jealous of this Laurie person."

Wylie laughed, but Amarina didn't.

"Hey, baby. She's just my mentor. Nothing else."

"What's she look like?"

"I don't know. Long dark hair."

"That's it? That's all you know?"

"I didn't pay a lot of attention, Amarina. I was trying to learn how not to die doing my job."

"I'm sorry."

"You need to relax, baby. I'm with you now. You're the only one that matters to me that way. She is critical to me at work, though. You need to accept that."

"I will. And I'll meet you guys for drinks tomorrow and I'll feel better."

"Sounds great." Wylie finished her beer. "Now, you ready for bed?"

Nothing would have made Wylie happier than crawling into bed and holding Amarina tight. But Amarina was in the mood for more, and Wylie also realized she had to prove herself to her. She was feeling insecure and Wylie felt that making love to her would solidify her affection for her. At least she hoped it would.

They walked into the bedroom and Wylie quickly removed Amarina's clothes.

"My God, you're beautiful," Wylie said. "I love your body."

"Thank you. I don't know what you see in me, but I'm glad you do."

"I see a beautiful, loving woman. A woman I want to spend all my time with."

Wylie climbed out of her clothes and they fell into bed. She slowly and tenderly made love to Amarina. She took her time and took her to several orgasms before she finally held her and they fell asleep.

The next morning, Wylie woke a little sore, but ready to dive again. Amarina dropped her off at the dock with the promise she'd meet her after work for drinks.

The day went smoothly for Wylie, but two other divers had to call it quits. After work, she joined the rest of the divers for a beer.

"My girlfriend is supposed to join us," she said.

"Girlfriend, eh?" Laurie said. "Lucky lady."

"Thanks. I'm actually the lucky one."

"Of course, you'd think so."

Wylie was on her second beer when she saw Amarina walk in. She stood and waved her over.

"Everyone, this is Amarina," she said. "Amarina, this is everyone."

Amarina stood self-consciously next to Wylie.

"Here. Let me grab you a chair," Laurie said. She took one from another table and set it between herself and Wylie.

"I'm Laurie, by the way. I've been Wylie's trainer for the past couple of days. Not that she needs much training. She's a natural."

"I'm glad to hear that," Amarina said. "I know she really enjoyed herself yesterday."

"She did really well today, too. I plan on having her picking up shells tomorrow."

"Right on," Wylie said. "I can't wait to get at it."

Wylie watched Amarina watching Laurie. She analyzed her herself. She had long brown hair, as she'd said, but that was all that was noticeable. She had green eyes, but they weren't outstanding or anything. Her nose was a little big and her mouth a little wide. Surely Amarina wouldn't be jealous now that she'd met her.

They stayed for a few more beers, then the group left en masse. Wylie took Amarina's hand as they walked to her car.

"Did you have fun?" she asked.

"I did," Amarina said. "You work with nice people."

"Yeah, I do. And that's important since I have to rely on them potentially having my back down there."

"Laurie seemed to really like you."

"She thinks I'm a good worker."

"I think it's more than that."

"She can like me all she wants," Wylie said. "My heart belongs to you."

"You say the sweetest things."

"I speak the truth, remember?"

"So you say."

"What do I need to do to convince you?"

"Nothing. I'm just being silly. I know that," Amarina said.

"Who do I go home with every night?"

"Me."

"Yep. Now let's get something to eat and head home."

True to her word, the next day, Laurie talked the captain into letting her train Wylie on picking up shells as they drifted. It was hard work and required concentration, plus there were times the boat kicked up so much mud Wylie couldn't see Laurie next to her. It was scary, but she just held on and kept breathing and it passed. The hardest part of the job was swimming her bag of shells over to the winch attached to the boat without letting go of her work line. She did it, but it wasn't easy.

By the end of the day, she was exhausted. But she had found one pearl, so that felt good. She went to the bar with everyone and Amarina was already there, since it had been her day off at the hostel. She walked over and kissed her and Amarina playfully pushed her away.

"You stink," she laughed. "You smell like fish."

"Imagine that," Wylie laughed, too.

"You get a shower as soon as we get home. Oh. And I went to the grocer's today so I'm cooking dinner."

"Sounds great. I could go for a nice hot shower and a good home-cooked meal."

They had several beers with the gang.

"I don't think I can lift another beer," Wylie finally said. "I'm wiped."

"Wuss," Laurie said.

The group laughed and Wylie said her good-byes. She and Amarina left hand in hand.

"So, was it as hard as you made it out to be?" Amarina asked when they got home.

"Harder."

"I'm sorry, babe. Why don't you hit the shower and I'll get dinner going?"

"Sounds great."

In the shower, Wylie could barely lift her hands above her head to shampoo, she was so sore. But the warm water felt good on her tired muscles. She contemplated while showering, that Amarina had never cooked for her before. This would be a treat.

She got out and dried off and put on some clean clothes. She wandered out to the kitchen to find Amarina hard at work. She walked up behind her and wrapped her arms around her.

"Do I smell better now?"

Amarina turned in her arms.

"Much."

Wylie kissed her, a kiss that started out soft, but soon turned to much more.

"Careful," Wylie said. "We may be skipping dinner if you keep that up."

"We don't want that to happen. Grab a beer and sit on the couch. Dinner's almost ready."

Wylie did as she was told. It felt good to be relaxing. Hanging with the other divers was nice, but just being home with Amarina felt right. It was an odd thing, her feeling that way, but she did. She pondered it briefly before Amarina announced dinner was ready.

They finished their dinner and Wylie started the dishes, but Amarina quickly sent her back to the couch.

"You had a rough day. I didn't work today. You rest."

Wylie sat on the couch and watched Amarina work in the kitchen. When Amarina was finished, she joined Wylie.

"Dinner was great," Wylie said. "I had no idea you could cook."

"That's because you're always taking me out to these fancy restaurants. You never gave me the chance."

"Well, you can cook whenever you like, baby. You know your way around a kitchen."

"Good. I'd like to do it more often. So you can come home and shower and relax for a little bit."

"I appreciate that."

"So, um, I'm guessing you're too tired for, you know…"

"Would you mind if I just held you tonight? I promise, I'll get used to this work in no time."

"No problem."

"Speaking of which, are you ready to hit the hay?"

"Sure thing."

Wylie crashed hard that night and didn't wake up until the alarm went off the next morning. She finished out her week with another three pearls, so was very happy with herself. She was also beaten to a pulp. She was glad when Friday afternoon arrived. After drinks with the gang, she and Amarina went home, Wylie showered, then collapsed on the couch. Amarina had to wake her for dinner.

When Wylie woke Saturday morning, Amarina was already at work. She stretched to work the kinks out of her tired muscles. She rolled over and checked the clock. Ten o'clock. Wow, she thought. She never slept past eight. Oh, well. She climbed out of bed and dressed slowly, then started her hike to the hostel.

By the time she reached it, her muscles felt better. She felt less sore. But when she walked in the lobby, Amarina was busy helping people with more people in line. Wylie went to the pool to kill some time. When she saw all the people leave the office, she walked in.

"Busy day today?" she said.

"You wouldn't believe it. But I knew all these people were coming today. I'd just forgotten. Clearly, I need to pay better attention to my job."

"You've been a little distracted, huh?" Wylie smiled.

"Just a little."

"I'd say I'm sorry."

"But you're not."

"No, I'm not."

"So, what are your plans for the day?" Amarina said.

"I don't really have any. I wanted to come see you, but I can't very well hang out here all day, can I?"

"Sure you can. As long as you get out of the way when people show up."

"Seriously?"

"Sure. I mean, you'll have to excuse me once in a while to do paperwork, like right now on the new people, but outside of that, I'm all yours."

"Right on. I'll stay here and talk to you then."

Wylie kept Amarina company all day and, when the day was finally over, took her out to dinner.

"You've been cooking for a while now, so I figured I'd take you to dinner."

"I've been cooking for three whole days." She laughed.

"Still. You deserve a day off."

They enjoyed their dinner out then drove home. Wylie was feeling frisky, as it had been several days since she'd enjoyed Amarina's body. As soon as they were in the house, she pulled her into her arms.

"I've missed you," she said.

"You've spent the whole day with me."

"That's not what I meant." She nuzzled Amarina's neck.

"Oh, my."

"Yeah?"

"Yeah."

Amarina pulled away and took Wylie's hand. She led her into the bedroom and started to undress.

"Slow down," Wylie said.

"Why?"

"Because you're sexy as hell, and I want to watch you do a striptease for me."

"Seriously?"

"Okay, not a striptease, but I want to watch you undress slowly."

"Okay. If that's what you want."

Wylie was sopping wet by the time Amarina stood naked in front of her.

"Come here, baby," she said.

Amarina came to stand by her. Wylie ran her hands over Amarina's breasts, down her sides, and to her hips.

"Damn, you're gorgeous."

"Shouldn't you get naked?" Amarina said.

"Yeah. I will. Let me admire you first." She pulled Amarina closer and held a breast while she took her nipple in her mouth. She tugged gently at first, then greedily as her need overtook her.

Amarina ran her fingers through Wylie's hair as she held her head in place.

"Babe?" she said. "I can't stand up much longer. My legs are shaking."

"Okay," Wylie said. She stood and quickly stripped out of her clothes. She pressed herself against Amarina and reveled in the feel of their naked bodies together.

"Damn, baby. You feel so good."

"Please can we lie down?"

"Sure. Yeah. We really need to."

Wylie laid down first and pulled Amarina on top of her. She bent her knee so Amarina could slide up and down her thigh. She loved the feel of her slickness as she did so.

"You're so wet," Wylie said.

"I need you." She rolled over onto her back and spread her legs. Wylie rolled on to her elbow and ran her hand over the length of Amarina's body.

"Your body is so sexy. I can't get over it."

"You make me feel sexy."

"You should."

Amarina grabbed Wylie's hand and placed it between her legs.

"Please," she said.

Wylie slid her hand along Amarina until she came to her center. She entered her as deeply as she could. With each thrust, she rubbed Amarina's clit with the base of her hand. She kept up with this and in no time could feel Amarina closing around her as she cried out.

Wylie moved down her body until she was where her legs met. She lowered her mouth and devoured the remnants of her orgasm, as well as all the new juices that flowed there. She licked circles around her clit before she took it in her mouth and sucked it hard while her tongue played over it. She was rewarded with another guttural scream as Amarina reached her climax.

She climbed up next to her, planning on holding Amarina, but she clearly had other plans. She kissed down Wylie's body until she was between her legs. She licked and sucked and soon Wylie was calling out her name as she came.

The next morning, they both had the day off so lounged around in bed, pleasing each other until about ten. Then Amarina sat up.

"Oh, my God. I completely forgot."

"Forgot what?"

"My parents are having a barbecue this afternoon. My whole family will be there. I told them about you and they said I could bring you."

"Seriously? You told them about me?"

"I did," Amarina said. "I told them I had a new friend I met at the hostel."

"I don't know. What if I go and they suspect something?"

"I don't think they will. I mean, why would they? We can act like we're just friends."

"Okay." Wylie tried to slow her racing heart. Meeting families was not her forte. She couldn't even remember the last time she'd met one. Had it been five, maybe ten years ago? "This is really important to you then?"

"Yes. I want you to meet them and I can't wait for them to meet you. They're going to love you, even if they don't know about us."

"Okay then. I can do this."

"What's wrong?"

"Nothing. It's just I'm not used to meeting families. But I'm really into you, so if this is important to you than this is what we'll do."

"I'll make it up to you," Amarina said as she rolled over on top of Wylie.

"I'm not really in the mood," Wylie said.

"Fine." Amarina pouted. "But later, okay?"

"Definitely later."

Chapter Fourteen

Wylie finished off her second beer.

"It's time, babe," Amarina said. "We really need to get going."

"Yeah. Okay. I'm ready."

They drove to Amarina's parents' house in silence. Wylie was a nervous wreck. The beers did nothing to calm her. She had no idea what to say to these people she'd never met.

"You're going to be fine," Amarina said as they pulled up in front of the two-story house.

"How many people are here?" Wylie looked around at all the cars.

"I have five brothers and two sisters, and I'm sure my parents invited some friends, as well."

Wylie thought she might have a panic attack. She had a hard time breathing, her palms were sweaty. She felt like she was going to pass out.

"You don't look good," Amarina said. "Should we bug out on this?"

"No. No. It's important to you, so we do it. I'll be fine."

She took a deep breath and calmed herself. She got out of the car and walked around to open Amarina's door for her. She braced herself one more time before they followed the stepping stones to the back yard. The place was crowded and she hoped her entrance with Amarina would go unnoticed. Such was not the case. A short, plump, middle-aged woman waved and hurried their way.

"Amarina! Amarina! I'm so glad you could make it." When she reached them, she extended her hand. "You must be Wylie."

"I am." Wylie smiled in spite of herself.

"I'm Amarina's mum. You can call me Mum. Everyone does."

Wylie looked at the woman in the flowered dress with the apron over it. She knew she was looking at Amarina in the future. She smiled easily.

"It's great to meet you…Mum."

Mum took her hand.

"Now come on. You must meet everybody. Amarina, you go get her something to drink while I take her around."

Wylie glanced back at a smiling Amarina as she was being led away. She was introduced to all Amarina's brothers and sisters and their spouses. Amarina was the only one still unwed, but as the baby of the family, that wasn't surprising.

Amarina finally joined them with beers as they were meeting Steven, Amarina's oldest brother.

"So, how long do you plan on staying in Broome?" he asked.

"Oh, dear," Mum said. "That's not something we need to worry about right now."

"Sure it is," Steven said. "I want to know if you're hanging around or leaving in a couple of weeks."

"Well, I had only planned on staying a few weeks, but now that I have a job, I can stay longer."

"How much longer?"

"Steven, please. Don't be rude," Mum said.

"I'm not being rude. I'm just making conversation."

"Well, come on, Wylie. You still need to meet Papa."

Papa was a tall, thin man also in an apron who was manning the barbecue.

"So you're Wylie," he said. "What a pleasure."

Wylie took his hand and shook it.

"It's a pleasure meeting you, too, sir."

"I need to manage the barbie, but I'll catch up with you later, okay?"

"Sounds good."

"I should get back to the kitchen," Mum said. "You two socialize, okay? Don't just stand in a corner."

"We won't," Amarina said.

When they were left alone, Amarina turned to Wylie.

"How you doing?"

"I'm okay. Most people here are really nice."

"Most?"

"Okay, all of them were nice. But I'm not sure Steven trusts me. And I think he's suspicious of us."

"Don't worry about him. What did he say, though?"

"He was questioning how long I'm staying."

"Ah. Why would he care?"

"That's why I think he suspects something," Wylie said. "He's your biggest big brother."

"That he is."

They mingled with others until Mum and Papa announced food was ready. They got in line for food and when they finally got theirs, the only open space left was next to Steven and his wife, Donna. Wylie felt a rock in the pit of her stomach as they walked over to sit down.

"Hey there," Wylie said as cheerfully as she could. "Are these seats taken?"

"Have a seat," Donna said.

"Thanks."

They sat down and began to eat.

"So," Steven said. "I'm still curious how long you plan to hang out and pretend to be mates with my sister."

"Steven!" Amarina said. "You're being rude. Don't use that tone with Wylie."

"No tone intended, Rina. I'm just asking a question. Surely you want to know the answer, too?"

"That's a conversation Wylie and I will have privately," Amarina said.

"Yeah, but when? As she's packing up to hit the road?"

Wylie started to speak, but Amarina stopped her.

"Don't say a thing, Wylie. He doesn't need to know anything. We'll have this talk when we're ready and not before."

Wylie nodded and went back to eating. It was hard, though, as her stomach had a huge knot in it. She wished she had an answer for Steven. Hell, she wished she had an answer for herself, but she didn't. She wasn't sure how long she'd be staying.

After the barbecue, they thanked Mum and Papa and said their good-byes and were driving home.

"I've been thinking," Amarina said.

"Yeah?"

"Why don't you give up your room at the hostel? It's costing you money and you're never there."

Wylie's stomach tightened again. That was like actually making a commitment. Could she do that? Then she told herself she was being ridiculous. That she was totally into Amarina and she was wasting money keeping her room at the hostel.

"That's a really good idea," she said.

"Let's go fill out the paperwork now."

"Sounds good. Everything I own that's not at your place is in my backpack, so I'll just grab it."

"Do you have your keys with you?"

"I do."

"Excellent. Oh. I'm so excited."

"Me, too." Wylie wasn't sure how excited she really was. This was a huge step. But it made sense, she kept telling herself.

Once they got her out of the hostel, they drove home.

Home, Wylie thought. Well, Northern California was still home, right? How long did she plan on staying in Broome? How long could she?

"You okay?" Amarina asked.

"Sure," Wylie said. "Long day. That's all."

"You sure?"

"Yep."

"I'm sorry if my family was too much for you."

"It wasn't really. They were all really nice."

"Except Steven."

"Yeah, well, he had his reasons. I know he knows about us. I could tell."

"I doubt it. If he did, he would have told Mum and Papa. The whole family would know."

They got out of the car and went inside. The air conditioner felt wonderful after having been outside all day. Wylie helped herself to a beer.

"You want one?" she asked Amarina.

"No, thanks. I'm full from dinner."

"Okay."

Wylie sat on the couch.

"Are you sure you're okay?" Amarina said. "You seem kind of distant."

"I'm fine."

"Is this about Steven? Really, I'm sorry for his behavior."

"No. He had every right to question me. It was no biggie, baby."

"Then what is it?"

"It's nothing. I promise."

"Okay."

They watched a movie together, then went to bed. Wylie made love to Amarina slowly and tenderly, making sure each touch let her know how much she meant to her. She didn't stop until Amarina insisted she was wiped out and could take no more.

They lay together after until Wylie heard the soft snoring, letting her know Amarina was asleep. Unable to sleep herself, she got up and went to the dining room table. She set her mind to figuring out her finances. She still had enough left from her original money to last another week, at least. She should have had enough for two weeks, but she hadn't planned on eating at all the restaurants she had been. The money she would make from pearl diving would be able to keep her there a while longer, at least. Probably as long as she wanted. But how long did she want? She dragged her hands over her face. What the hell was she doing? She'd just effectively moved in with Amarina. Which was great, except how long would it last? How long could it last? She was crazy about her, but she had a whole other life in California. Could she just walk away from that?

She heard footsteps behind her and felt Amarina's hands on her shoulders.

"What's up?" Amarina said.

"I couldn't sleep."

"What's going on?" Amarina sat next to her at the table. "Talk to me."

"Nothing serious. I was just calculating how much money I have left."

"You know, your money would last a lot longer if we didn't eat out all the time."

"I know," Wylie said. "And we haven't been. You've been cooking."

"We need to keep that up."

They sat silently for a few minutes.

"So, what's really the point? To see how long you can stay? Do we really want to have this conversation in the middle of the night? We should go back to bed. We both have to work in the morning."

"Okay," Wylie said. "Let's go back to bed."

She was finally able to fall asleep, but not after tossing and turning for a quite a while.

Five fifteen came awfully early. Wylie dragged herself out of bed and found her board shorts and T-shirt in the dark. She was on her second cup of coffee when Amarina came into the kitchen.

"How ya doing this morning?" Amarina asked.

"I'm tired. You?"

"Tired. But I'll survive. I don't have to drift along the ocean floor looking for oysters."

"I'll be fine, baby. Don't worry."

"I have to worry. It's my job."

Wylie smiled. It was nice to have someone to worry about her. She wasn't used to it, but it sure felt good.

"We should get going," Amarina said.

Wylie got out of the car just as the main boat was pulling up to the dock. She took a deep breath and steadied herself for what she knew was going to be a very long day.

She survived the day and even managed to find three pearls. Each pearl was extra money, so she was very pleased with herself. She thought she'd be able to think a little on her breaks, but she was too busy catching her breath and cleaning shells to really ponder her situation.

She came into the kitchen after her shower that night to find a nice bottle of wine on the counter and a wonderful smelling spaghetti dinner ready for them.

"This looks fancy," Wylie said. "What's the occasion?"

"I thought we could talk while we eat."

"Talk about what?"

"What do you think?"

Wylie's chest tightened. She wasn't ready to talk about things yet. She'd already made a commitment to Amarina. But how much of one could she make? Long term wasn't her style. Yet the idea of leaving Amarina made her chest tighten more.

Amarina served them then took her place next to Wylie. Wylie poured them each a glass of wine. She took a sip.

"This is good."

"It should be," Amarina said.

"How much was it?"

"Are we ready to talk finances with each other?"

Wylie sat back. She exhaled.

"I suppose we are."

"Good."

"So, I have enough money to stay for about a week, maybe a week and a half. But I'm making bank diving so I should easily be able to afford to stay longer."

"I'm not charging you rent, so that should help," Amarina said.

"It will."

"So, the question that everyone wants to know the answer to is how long you're going to stay."

"I'm thinking about contacting my bosses and letting them know I'm going to stay another month. We'll see how it goes from there. So, I guess the bottom line is, I still don't know. I do know I'll stay as long as I can."

"I really like you, Wylie."

"I really like you, too."

"I want you to know, I'm not playing some game. I'm not like Kathryn or any of the other women you've been with."

Wylie took her hand.

"Good God, no you're not. I know this. I don't think of you like that at all. Believe me."

"And yet you're treating me like one."

"How so?"

"You're stringing me along, Wylie. And I don't like it."

"I'm sorry, Amarina. I don't have an answer. I wish I did. I promise to text my boss tomorrow and let him know I won't be back for a while."

"And what happens then? That's what I want to know."

"I can't say. Let's just see how it's going after a month, okay?"

"Okay. Fine. Whatever. I don't see my feelings changing, but I'm sure there's a chance you'll get tired of me. Or maybe Laurie'll look more appealing."

"Stop it, please. You know I'm not into Laurie and I never will be. I'm going to do all I can to stay with you."

They finished their dinner in tense silence. After, Wylie did the dishes while Amarina watched television. When the kitchen was clean, Wylie joined Amarina on the couch.

"So, are you never speaking to me again?"

"I'm just frustrated is all."

"So am I."

"But you can control things. I can't. I just have to sit around and hope you somehow decide I'm worth being with."

CHAPTER FIFTEEN

I'm sorry, Amarina. I really am. I just can't say right now how long I'll be staying."

"Whatever."

"No, not whatever."

"If you want me to say it's okay, that I don't mind waiting to see if I become a priority to you then you're going to be disappointed, because I won't say that."

"You are a priority to me, baby. I don't know how to make you see that."

"Whatever," Amarina said again, "I'm going to bed."

"Yeah. Let's get some sleep on this and things will look better in the morning."

They lay there, each on their own side of the bed, staring at the ceiling. Wylie reached for Amarina's hand. Amarina kept her hand limp, but let Wylie hold it.

Wylie rolled over and faced Amarina.

"I promise I'll get an extra month," she said. "I promise to text my boss tomorrow."

"But what about after that? That's what I care about. That's what I'm worried about. A month comes and goes and you decide you don't want to play house with me anymore. Then you'll leave me. And I'm not going to lie to you. That's going to hurt."

"I'm not 'playing house' with you, baby. Come on. Surely you know that."

"It's what it feels like. I can't help that."

"There's more to my decision, baby. I need some help from you. I'm not used to living in a closet. You know that."

"Don't put this all on me."

"I'm not putting it all on you. But I'm saying part of me staying will have to be contingent on you coming out."

Silence. No more words were uttered that night.

Wylie was getting her coffee the next morning when Amarina walked into the kitchen. Wylie had been thinking long and hard about how to proceed and she came up with one solution. It was not the solution she wanted, but it was what she felt she needed to present Amarina with.

She sat at the dining room table.

"I've been thinking," she said.

"That's a start." Amarina sat next to her at the table.

"Baby, it kills me to ask this, but do you want me to move back to the hostel? Would that be better?"

Amarina stood.

"How can you even say such a thing? Where did that come from?"

"You say you feel like we're playing house. I feel horrible that you don't take me seriously. I was just wondering if moving out would be what you want."

"No! I want you here with me. Are you crazy? That's the whole point. I want you with me. Not just for a month or two. That's where the problem is. It's not that I *don't* want you here. What were you thinking?"

"I don't know. I guess I wasn't. I just thought…"

"You thought you'd just dump me now, is that it?"

"I don't want to dump you, Amarina. Please. I want to be with you."

"Fine. Let's quit fighting. You stay an extra month and then we'll play it by ear. If I only get one more month with you, it's better than nothing. I guess."

"Thanks, baby. And who knows what's going to happen after that?"

"Okay, well, we need to get going or you're going to miss your boat."

They arrived just as the boat did. Wylie had to run to get on it before it took off. Her day was rough. She was bumped along the bottom and ended up ripping the elbow of her wetsuit. Her elbow bled and she was terrified it would draw the attention of sharks. She was more grateful than ever when it was break time.

They dressed her wound and the bleeding stopped. She was ready to go again. At the end of the day, she had one pearl and a thrashed elbow. Not much to write home about. She begged off of drinking with the gang, opting instead to go meet Amarina at the hostel. While she was waiting for her to get off work, she texted her boss back in California, letting him know she was planning on staying another month. She got a text back approving her additional time off.

"So, my boss says I can take another month off," she said, all smiles.

"That's great."

"Yep. We should go out to celebrate."

"I swear, Wylie Boase, nobody likes to spend money like you do."

"I do, indeed. But this calls for celebration, right?"

"You're right. You've got to get out of those stinky clothes, though. By the way, why is there a bandage on your elbow?"

"Things got a little rough at work today."

"Looks like that might be an understatement."

"Yeah. It hurt like a mother. But it's fine."

Amarina finished her shift and they walked to her car.

"Are you sure you don't want me just to fix some dinner?" she said.

"I'm sure. I want to party. I'll take a quick shower and then we'll head out."

Her shower was quick, though it took longer than she'd anticipated since she had to be careful washing her elbow. It hurt like crazy and started bleeding again in the shower. She got out and had Amarina help her apply a new bandage.

"Was it bleeding like this in the water?" Amarina asked.

"Yeah."

"Do you know there are sharks in the water?"

"I realize that, baby. I wasn't in the water long with it bleeding. My break time came shortly after I did this. And then we got the bleeding stopped during my break."

"You put the whole dive team in danger, didn't you?"

"Jesus, Amarina. It's not like I did it on purpose."

"Oh, no. I didn't mean to be accusatory. It's just kind of sinking in how dangerous it was."

"Oh. Okay. Yeah. It was a very serious situation."

"And yet you want to continue doing it?"

"Of course. It was a one-time thing. I'm not worried about having a repeat performance."

They went out for dinner, where Wylie insisted they both have margaritas.

"We both have to work tomorrow," Amarina protested.

"We won't have too many. Just a couple. Believe me, I'm not going to try to dive for pearls hung over. Oh my God, would that be a mistake."

"Yeah, you'd be bloody all over."

"Not necessarily, but it certainly wouldn't be fun. I can just imagine a pounding head to go along with the whoosh, whoosh, whoosh the propeller makes. I'd probably lose my lunch."

"That would attract all kinds of fish, I'd imagine."

"Oh yeah. I don't want to think about it."

They finished dinner and held hands as they walked back to the car.

"So, are we good now?" Wylie said.

"Yeah. For now. I'm still wondering about the long term, but I've decided to just take this one day at a time."

"Excellent. One day at a time it is. And each day is followed by a night. And I like the idea of taking things one night at a time." She smiled and wiggled her eyebrows.

"You need to be careful with that elbow," Amarina said.

"Oh, I will be. You just need to relax. I'll take care of everything."

"I'm sure you will."

They got back to the cottage and Wylie started taking Amarina's clothes off as soon as the door was closed behind them.

"Wylie," Amarina said quietly. "The neighbors."

Sure enough, the blinds were open. Wylie quickly closed them and went back to undressing Amarina. She peeled her shirt off and kissed the exposed skin. She made herself go slowly, even though she longed to rip Amarina's clothes off her and have her way with her.

She unzipped and lowered Amarina's shorts and Amarina stepped out of them. She peeled off her underwear and Amarina stood naked in front of her.

Wylie eased her onto the couch and climbed on top of her. She kissed her hard before she slid lower and took a nipple in her mouth. She placed her hands between her legs and stroked her clit, which was slick and ready for her. It didn't take much time at all for Amarina to climax.

"Let's go to bed," Amarina said.

Wylie stood and walked down the hall to the bedroom. She quickly took off her own clothes and lay on the bed where Amarina joined her. She climbed between Wylie's legs and pleased her until she was a bundle of tension just waiting to erupt. When she could take no more, the tension exploded and Wylie had one orgasm after another that cascaded over her.

They continued to take things one day at a time, spending time together on Sundays and enjoying each other to the fullest in their nights together. Nothing more was mentioned about what might happen at the end of the month.

Wylie continued her success as a pearl diver. She had a lot of fun doing it, and had an uncanny ability to find shells with pearls in them. It wasn't all fun and games, though. She knew how dangerous diving was, what with the predatory sharks and the jellyfish. But it really came to light when Laurie was stung by an Irukandji jellyfish. She was mere feet from Wylie. It could easily have been her instead.

They got Laurie out of the water and performed the first stages of medical treatment on her. Soon it became apparent she needed a hospital, so they pulled all the divers out and got the boom back to the main boat. They proceeded to the dock, where an ambulance was waiting for her.

After, the boat took the boomer back out and the divers went back to work. Business as usual. But Wylie was plenty shaken. She was extra paranoid on the rest of her runs that day.

The group that met at the pub that afternoon was small and sullen. Some of the divers had gone to the hospital to see Laurie. The ones who stayed were quiet.

Amarina showed up.

"What's going on? Where is everybody?"

"They're at the hospital. Laurie got stung by an Irukandji today."

"Oh, my God. That's horrible. How is she?"

"Well, they couldn't do anything for her on the boat. They needed to take her to the hospital."

"That's so scary. And she dives right next to you, doesn't she?"

"Yeah. It was a close call. I'm well aware of how lucky I was today."

Amarina hugged her.

"Oh wow. Now I'm going to worry every time you dive. I mean, worry more. I already worry about you with bleeding arms and sharks and all of that."

"Would you mind if we swung by the hospital to see her?" Wylie said. She hesitated to ask because she knew how jealous Amarina could be, but she felt the need to check in on Laurie.

"Not at all. Let's go get you cleaned up first."

They said their good-byes to the group and went home so Wylie could shower and change. They drove to the hospital. Amarina was silent on the drive.

"You know I just want to go out of concern for a coworker. It's nothing more than that. You know that, right?" Wylie said.

"I understand," Amarina said sharply. "I'm not convinced. But I'm trying to be strong and not let my jealousy take over. It's not easy, Wylie. But I'm trying."

"She was stung by a venomous jellyfish. She had to be taken to the hospital. This isn't something I want to do just to see Laurie.

It's something I need to do to make sure she's okay. I'll be diving with these jellyfish every day, Amarina. I need to be sure she's okay or I'm going to be preoccupied on every dive. And that's not safe. It could be deadly."

They arrived at the hospital and Wylie was a bundle of nerves. She knew how bad these stings could be and she had no idea what to expect when they walked in. They inquired at the front desk and were told to wait in the waiting room until some of the visitors had left, as there were too many in with her already.

Wylie paced nervously, occasionally chancing a glance over at Amarina who sat watching her. She sat next to her.

"I'm sorry to make us do this, baby. I just really need to see how she's doing."

"That's fine. I'm thinking about just leaving though. Maybe I'll go home and make dinner and come back later to pick you up."

"Please don't. I need you here for support."

"Are you sure you wouldn't want to be alone with her?"

"Amarina, don't."

"I told you it wouldn't be easy for me."

"You also told me you'd try."

"Okay. I'll stay."

Two people came out of Laurie's room which meant Wylie and Amarina could go in.

"Do I have to ask you to come in with me?" Wylie said.

"Oh no. I'm coming."

She took Wylie's hand and held it tight.

They walked into the room to find Laurie hooked up to IVs and somewhat out of it.

"How's she doing?" Wylie asked one of the other divers.

"They said we got her here in time. She's on pain medication and something else in her IV. I don't remember what he said, but it's supposed to make her better."

"How long will she be in here?"

"They think she'll be able to go home tomorrow."

"That's a relief."

"Yeah it is. Hey, mate, lucky for you that jelly wasn't a few feet to the right, eh?"

"You're not kidding. I'm glad she's going to be okay."

Wylie touched Laurie's arm and felt Amarina's grip on her hand tighten.

"Laurie?" she said. "Can you hear me?"

Laurie looked at her and opened her eyes.

"I'm glad you're gonna be okay, mate," Wylie said.

"Me, too," Laurie managed.

"Get some rest and I'll see you in a few days?"

Laurie nodded.

Wylie said good-bye to the other divers and left the hospital with Amarina still having a death grip on her hand.

"See? That wasn't so bad. I just needed to know she was going to be okay. If I get stung now, I'll know I'll spend maybe a day in the hospital and then I'll be good to go. That's a good thing, right?"

"I'd rather you not get stung at all."

"I'd rather that, too, but if it happens, I'll know what to expect. I was terrified walking in there, Amarina. Do you know that? I was scared shitless to see what kind of shape Laurie would be in. I was terrified they'd say they needed to amputate or worse. I needed to do this for my own peace of mind."

"I get it. I do. And I'm glad you can put your mind at rest. But I still want you to be extra careful."

"Always, baby. I'm always careful down there. Especially since I scraped my elbow, I've been careful."

They stopped for a bite to eat and were both preoccupied. Wylie was withdrawn, as she thought about Laurie. She realized halfway through the meal that they hadn't spoken to each other.

"Penny for your thoughts?" she said.

"I'm just leaving you alone with your thoughts. You seemed like you needed that."

"I appreciate that, baby, but I think I'd rather talk to you. You know, to distract me. How was your day?"

"It was quiet. Running a hostel isn't as exciting as diving for pearls."

"No? You're lucky. I'd love to have a mellow job."

"You would not," Amarina laughed. "You love your job and you know it."

"Yeah. I guess I'm just shaken after today. I really do love every aspect of diving."

They got home and turned on the television. They snuggled against each other while watching a movie. Before the movie was over, Wylie had to have Amarina. She needed to prove to herself that she was alive and fine and that Amarina was alive as well.

She slid her hand down in front of Amarina's shoulder until it caressed one of her full breasts.

"What are you doing?" Amarina said.

"What does it feel like?"

"I like the way it feels."

"Good. Help me out here. Unbutton your shirt for me."

Amarina did as she was asked. Wylie reached down into her bra and pulled her breast out. She teased her nipple until it stood hard. She moved her hand to her other breast and did the same. She kissed the back of Amarina's neck and nibbled on the side of it.

"What's gotten into you?" Amarina asked.

"Nothing. I just need you. I need you right now."

"Mind you, I'm not complaining. I just thought after everything that happened today..."

"Everything that happened today reminded me you never know when you're time's up. You've got to take advantage of every second you can while you're alive."

"Well then, by all means, don't let this moment pass you by."

CHAPTER SIXTEEN

I won't," Wylie said. She stood from the couch and offered a hand to Amarina. They walked back to their bedroom. She unhooked Amarina's bra so her breasts fell free.

Unencumbered by the bra, they were much easier for Wylie to knead, tease and suck. She took her time, drawing out each moment. She buried her face between Amarina's breasts and rubbed them on her cheeks. She kissed one, then the other, then both again.

"Damn, you've got to be the sexiest woman I've ever met," Wylie said when she came up for air.

"You're so sweet."

"No, I mean it. I can't get enough of you."

"Well, take me. Take all of me."

"Oh, I will, baby. You know I will."

Wylie continued to kiss from breast to breast while she pinched Amarina's nipples. She knew it wouldn't take long and in a couple of minutes, Amarina was coming for her.

"I love how responsive you are, baby. I love knowing everything I do to you, for you, with you, makes you come."

"I love what you do to me. Please don't stop."

"Oh, I won't stop. I'm not about to stop."

She took Amarina's nipple in her mouth again as she skimmed her hand over her body.

"We need to get you out of these shorts," she finally said.

Amarina stood and together, they got her shorts off. Wylie stripped out of her clothes as well. They lay back down together and

Wylie went back to what she was doing. She was committing every inch of Amarina to memory. Her hand covered every curve, every delicious curve, before slipping between her legs.

She stroked her lightly and teased her. She wanted to draw it out, make it last. She wanted Amarina to have to wait to climax. It didn't matter. Amarina came almost immediately.

Wylie laughed.

"I'm trying to draw this out for you," she said.

"I can't help it. You get me so turned on."

Wylie dipped her fingers inside her then and stroked her walls. Again, the climax hit within minutes. Wylie kissed down Amarina's body, stopping to lick and nibble here and there on her way to where her legs met. She climbed between them and rested her cheek on her cool inner thigh.

"You're beautiful," she said.

"I'm so lucky you think so."

"Oh, baby, I do. God, you're just beautiful."

Wylie moved her mouth to Amarina's clit and licked it. She sucked it gently before shifting her mouth to lick inside her. She heard Amarina's breathing getting shallow, so she moved back to her clit. She took it in her mouth again and ran her tongue over it. Amarina cried out several times as the orgasms rolled over her.

Wylie didn't let up until Amarina tapped her head.

"No more," she said. "Are you trying to kill me?"

"What a way to go, huh?" Wylie said. She climbed up next to Amarina and collapsed, exhausted.

"No doubt. Man, you sure know how to love me up."

"That's my job, baby. Taking care of you in any way is my job."

"Well, you do it so well."

"Good. Now, come here and let me hold you."

"I don't think so. Let me gain my strength and then you shall reap the rewards of me taking care of you as well."

Wylie wasn't about to complain. She was one giant nerve ending. Every inch of her tingled with desire. The slightest touch from Amarina was sure to send her rocketing into the atmosphere.

Amarina soon caught her breath and ran her hands over Wylie's breasts. Wylie gasped at the feeling. She needed Amarina more than she'd ever needed anyone. She would try to hold off as long as she could, but Amarina's caresses were tender and loving and just what she needed.

When she felt Amarina's hand skim over her slick clit, she grit her teeth in an effort not to come too soon.

"You can't fight it," Amarina said. "You know you need release."

"I'll hold off as long as I can," Wylie managed.

"Don't babe. Let it go. I want you to come for me."

Wylie relaxed and let the sensations flow over her. She'd needed that orgasm. But Amarina wasn't through. She ran her fingers over Wylie's clit again, and pressed it into her pubis. Again, Wylie had to let go and let it happen.

"You make me feel so good, baby."

"Good. You keep on relaxing and we'll keep on having fun."

"You got it."

Amarina slid her fingers deep inside Wylie.

"How does that feel?"

"It feels amazing, but I need more."

"More?"

Amarina slid another finger in. She pulled them all the way out before she plunged them back in. Each thrust pushed them in deeper. Soon Wylie was writhing on the bed, gripping the sheets.

"Oh, baby. Oh, yes. Oh, dear God yes."

Then she grew silent. The whole room was silent save for the sound of Amarina's fingers. And then it hit. The hardest orgasm she'd ever experienced crashed over her and took her on wave after wave of pleasure.

"Oh, baby," she said when she could finally speak. "That was fucking amazing. Oh, my God."

Amarina snuggled close to her.

"I'm glad I could make you feel good."

"Good? Baby, you made me feel *great*."

"Good. I want to always make you feel that way."

"You will, baby. You will," Wylie said before slipping off to sleep.

The morning came early, too early for Wylie's liking. She got up and dressed then made her way to the kitchen for coffee. She was shaking a little bit from being so tired. That wasn't a good sign. She sat at the table and took a deep breath. She willed herself to calm down. She couldn't be shaking at work. She sipped some more coffee and the shaking settled a little. Was she scared? Was that what the shaking was from? She hoped not. She couldn't afford it.

Amarina got up and came out to join her for coffee.

"How are you this morning?" Amarina said.

"I'm okay."

"Only okay? Clearly I did something wrong."

"Oh no, baby," Wylie said. "You did everything right. I just seem to have the shakes this morning and I'm not sure what's up with that."

"It's natural that you'd be a little scared to go back in the water today, Wylie. But you'll be fine. You have to believe that."

"I do. I know I'll be fine. But I still have the shakes. They've got to go away before I get in the water."

"They will. Do you want some more coffee?"

"Please."

She sipped the coffee and tried to relax. She was feeling better when the time came for them to leave.

"You ready?" Amarina said. "You're going to be late."

"I'm ready." She took another deep breath and stood.

They got to the dock a little early, for which Wylie was grateful. She wanted a little more time to get over the shakes and the butterflies that had taken up residence in her stomach before she had to dive.

She kissed Amarina good-bye and got out of the car. The group of divers on the dock were quiet. There was no boisterous joking that usually went on before a dive.

"Has anyone heard how Laurie is?" Wylie asked.

"She's doing great. No worries, mate."

"Good."

Wylie's nerves didn't calm down, especially when she was at the bottom of the ocean and the spot next to her, Laurie's spot, was empty. She tried not to focus on that, but she did and ended up ripping her knee on a shell. The blood poured forth and Wylie had to be pulled up, as well as the other divers on her boom. There was no reason for them to stay down there with the sharks.

After an appropriate amount of time, during which Wylie's knee was tended to, the divers were allowed back in the water. Wylie was extra careful and ended the day with the fewest shells she'd ever collected. There were no pearls for her that day.

"You had a bad day, Boase," the captain said to her.

"Yes, ma'am."

"I need you to step it up tomorrow. I was hoping you'd make up for Laurie not being here. But you didn't. I need you to really help make up for her loss and now your bad day. Do you understand?"

"Yes, ma'am."

"Good."

The boom met up with the main boat and the journey back to the dock began. The rest of the group were loud and carefree, seeming to have forgotten Laurie and the scare the day before. She tried to join in their revelry but couldn't bring herself to. She was still preoccupied with it and now she had a painful knee to go with it. She couldn't bend it, what with the stitches they'd used to close the wound. It hurt.

"You going to the pub with us, Wylie?" someone said.

"No. I'm going to go meet my girl and go home and take it easy."

"Okay. Take care of that knee."

"I will."

She hobbled down to the hostel. Amarina took one look at her limping and came out from behind the counter.

"What happened?"

"I cut my leg on a shell."

"How bad is it?"

"They had to stitch it up," Wylie said.

"Oh, baby. I'm so sorry."

"It's okay. It'll heal."

"Still…Okay, let me finish up here and we'll head home."

"Thanks."

As it turned out, Amarina's replacement was late, so Wylie had to sit in the office an extra half hour. Her clothes had dried and the sand and salt in them chafed her skin. When he finally got there, Amarina took him into the back office presumably to rip him a new one. When they came out, he looked properly chastised and she grabbed her purse.

"Come on, Wylie. Let's get you home."

Wylie was glad to get out of there. She just wanted a shower and a drink.

"Do we have any Scotch at your place?" she asked.

"No."

"Can we stop and get some?"

"Sure. We can do anything you need."

Wylie leaned her head against the headrest and closed her eyes. Her knee was throbbing and she was exhausted.

Amarina ran into the liquor store and came out with a bottle of Scotch for Wylie. They then continued their journey home. Once there, Wylie hobbled up the stone pathway to the front door. Sore and stiff, she made it to the kitchen, where she opened the bottle of Scotch and poured herself a glass. She took two ibuprofen with the first swig.

"You should get in the shower, babe," Amarina said. "Do you need any help?"

"Yeah. I'll probably need help getting my shorts off."

"Well, why don't we go do that now? You'll feel better when you're clean."

They went back to the bathroom and Wylie took her T-shirt off. She leaned against the sink counter while Amarina pulled off her shorts.

"I'll take these outside and hose them off," Amarina said. "You enjoy your shower."

Wylie stood in the shower and let the warm water wash over her. It felt good and she was in no hurry to get out. She finally grabbed a washcloth and washed the dirt of the day off her body. When she was clean, she carefully stepped out of the tub and dried off.

With just a towel wrapped around her waist, she walked back to the kitchen and took another sip of Scotch.

Amarina came in from the yard and stopped in the living room.

"Well, that's a lovely sight," she said. "You sure know how to make a girl's heart go pitter-patter."

"Sorry. I just didn't feel like getting dressed. I don't even know if I can without your help."

"Well, I'll be happy to help you. Though I do like the sight of you naked."

"I have a towel wrapped around my waist."

"I can't see that from here." She laughed.

"Okay, then. Let your imagination run wild."

"Don't worry. It is."

"Mm. Good. Since your imagination is the only thing that will enjoy my nudity tonight, unfortunately."

"Oh, babe, I understand. I wouldn't expect anything else. But I can still enjoy the view, right?"

"Definitely."

"Do you want to get dressed, though? I mean, in all seriousness?" Amarina asked.

"I'd like to put on some boxers and an undershirt, yes."

"Okay. Well, let me go get some. You stay right where you are."

Wylie was happy to oblige. She topped off her Scotch and shifted her weight off her bad leg. Amarina was back in a moment. She knelt on the ground and opened up the boxers so Wylie could put her leg through the hole. She helped her with her other leg, then pulled them up. Wylie slipped the undershirt over her head.

"I'm going to put the towel in the bathroom," Amarina said. "Why don't you sit on the sofa and put your leg up?"

"Excellent idea."

Wylie limped to the couch. She eased herself down onto it and put her foot up on the coffee table. She leaned back. That felt much better.

"You doing okay then?" Amarina asked.

"Much better. Thanks."

"Do you mind if I help myself to a nip of your Scotch?"

"Of course not. You don't even have to ask. Help yourself."

Amarina poured a glass and came and sat next to Wylie.

"So, Danger Girl. Did something else happen today that you're not telling me about?"

"Nothing serious."

"Something that's got you preoccupied though," Amarina said.

"I kind of got in trouble today."

"For getting cut?"

"After I cut my knee, I got really cautious," Wylie said. "So, my take was low. It was the lowest it's ever been. And the captain said she'd expected me to make up for Laurie not being there. She was really disappointed in me."

"Accidents happen. Surely she knows that."

"She does. I'm sure. But it's her job to bring in pearls. And it's our jobs to make sure she has those pearls to bring in."

"Oh, well. One bad day isn't the end of the world."

"She wants me to go apeshit tomorrow to make up for today and for Laurie's absence tomorrow."

"But you need to be careful," Amarina said. "Especially now with your knee cut."

"I can't be too careful tomorrow, baby. I am gonna need to just go for it."

"I don't like the sound of that. I'm going to worry all day. Maybe I'll make you stay home with me tomorrow."

Wylie laughed.

"That's not going to happen. You need not to worry. I'll be fine."

"Well, clearly you're worried about it. If you can worry, I can, too."

"I'm sorry," Wylie said. "I shouldn't have said anything."

"Yes, you should have. I'm glad you did. It's important for me to know what's going on with you."

"I should have kept it to myself."

"No. You were totally preoccupied. I would have pestered you until I got it out, so it's just as well you were honest right off."

"I suppose that's true."

"Yes, it is," Amarina said. "Now, you relax and I'll make dinner."

They ate in the living room so Wylie could keep her leg up. After dinner, they watched a movie, during which Wylie fell asleep. She awoke to Amarina gently nudging her.

"Wylie? Babe? Come on. Let's get you to bed."

Wylie stood and found her leg very stiff. She limped to the bedroom and fell into bed. When she woke the next morning, her leg was throbbing. She wanted nothing more than to climb back into bed and blow off the day's work. But she couldn't and she knew that. The captain was expecting great things from her that day and she was determined to perform.

She took a couple of ibuprofen with her first cup of coffee and sat down at the table. She looked at her knee and saw that it was swollen and bruised. Not a good sign. Not a bad sign, for sure. Nothing to be worried about, but not a sign that it would be feeling better by the end of the day.

Amarina woke up and joined her.

"Will you need help getting dressed?" she asked.

"Probably."

"I'll go get your things."

Wylie had a second cup of coffee while she waited. She was starting to feel better. It was going to be a long day, but she would manage. Amarina came in and helped Wylie out of her boxers and into her board shorts.

"Good thing you don't have to bend your knee to skim the bottom," Amarina said.

"Tell me about it. As a matter of fact, if I'd kept my knee straight yesterday, I wouldn't be in this predicament."

"Well, I want you to be extra careful today. I don't care what Captain Hardass has to say."

CHAPTER SEVENTEEN

Amarina dropped Wylie off at the dock with one more admonishment to be careful. Wylie took her time as she hobbled toward the group on the dock.

"How ya doin' mate?" someone asked.

"I'll be okay," Wylie said.

"You look a little unsteady on your feet."

"It's just a little limp. Nothing that'll affect me in the water."

"Good to hear. I'd hate you to get hurt worse."

"Nah. I'll be fine."

Wylie needed help getting into her wetsuit, but once she was in it, she forced herself to forget about the pain and focus only on picking up shells. And pick up shells she did. At the end of the day, she'd set a new record for shells. Everyone was congratulating her on a job well done.

"You did good today," the captain said. "Real good."

"Thank you."

"And how many pearls did you get?"

"Four."

"Four? In a day? Not a bad day for you at all. Thank you for stepping up, Boase."

"No worries, ma'am. It needed to happen."

"How's your knee?" the captain asked.

"It's sore, but I'll live."

"Get those stitches removed next Monday, okay?"

"Will do."

The boom met up with the boat.

"See you tomorrow, Boase."

"See you tomorrow."

Wylie stepped carefully from the boom to the boat. The surface of each was wet, and she didn't want to fall. She started to slip, but another diver saw and caught her before she went down.

"Thank you," she said.

"No worries."

Wylie was thankful she'd bent her left knee and not her right. She'd hate to blow out all the stitches. She checked the bandage and it was still clean. She had nothing to worry about.

Amarina was waiting at the pub when the gang arrived. Wylie limped in, favoring her right leg.

"How was your day?" Amarina asked.

"It was great," Wylie said. "I set a record for shells and found four pearls. It was an awesome day."

Someone passed a beer her way.

"To the shell master," he said.

Everyone raised their glasses and cheered her. She took a long pull.

"Here," she said to Amarina. "You have a seat and I'll go get you a beer, too."

"No, I'm fine. Too much Scotch for me last night. Thanks, though. Has anyone heard from Laurie?" she asked the group.

"She'll be back to work tomorrow," someone said.

"Wow. That's a quick recovery isn't it?" Amarina said.

"She doesn't really have a choice. She needs the money. Plus she's feeling better."

"Man, she's got to be gun-shy getting back in that water," Wylie said.

"You did it," Amarina said.

"I have a few stitches in my knee. I didn't end up in the hospital."

"True that, mate," one of the divers said. "Still, Laurie's a tough one. Good stock in that one. If she thinks she's ready, she is."

"Well, I'll be happy to have her back," Wylie said.

"I bet you will."

Amarina squeezed Wylie's hand and she knew she'd heard enough about Laurie.

"You ready to go?" Wylie asked her.

"Sure. If you are."

"We're going to take off, mates. Thanks for the beer."

"Take care of that leg."

"Will do."

Amarina didn't let go of Wylie's hand until they were in the parking lot.

"How are you really?" Amarina asked.

"I'm sore and exhausted, to be honest."

"I'm sorry. But I've got a roast going in the slow cooker. Dinner should be ready soon. You can have another nice, quiet evening."

"Oh, baby. That sounds wonderful."

They got home and Amarina helped Wylie out of her shorts again and Wylie took another long, hot shower. She managed to get her boxers on and even put a pair of shorts on over them. She threw a T-shirt on and went to the kitchen, where Amarina was serving up the pot roast.

"It smells delicious," Wylie said. She poured herself a glass of Scotch and took her plate to the table.

"You sure you don't want to eat in the living room again? You can put your leg up."

"I'll do that after dinner. Thanks, though."

They chatted as they ate. Amarina had visited her mum that day.

"The whole family really enjoyed meeting you," she said.

"Everyone except Steven," Wylie said.

"Don't start that again."

"Okay. Sorry. I enjoyed meeting all of them, too. And how is Mum doing?"

"She's great. She wants to have us over again. Sometime when it's just the two of them."

"That sounds like fun. Let's do that."

"Great. How does Sunday sound?"

"Sounds great. We'll plan on it."

They moved to the couch after dinner and Wylie put her leg up and leaned her head back. She closed her eyes and took a deep breath. She hurt. She was tired of pretending she didn't. Her leg was killing her and every muscle in her body ached from what she'd put her body through that day. She dozed off.

Amarina woke her.

"Hey babe, do you want to go to bed?"

"What time is it?"

"Eight."

"No," Wylie laughed. "I think I've got at least another hour in me."

"Okay. If you're sure."

"Sure. Now put on something fun to watch and let's just veg."

Amarina found a sitcom to watch and settled in next to Wylie.

"This is one of my favorites," Wylie said.

They watched together for another half hour before Wylie felt her eyelids getting heavy.

"Baby?" she said.

"Hm?"

"Let's go to bed."

"Okay."

Wylie woke the next morning needing Amarina. She reached over and ran her hand over her body and brought it to stop on a breast. She softly kneaded it then circled it before she lightly pinched her nipple.

"What are you doing?" Amarina said.

"What does it feel like?"

"It feels like you're going to be late for work."

"No, I won't. I can be quick."

"You can, huh?"

"Yep."

Wylie climbed between Amarina's legs and licked the length of her. She focused her licking on Amarina's clit and Amarina cried out almost immediately. Wylie kept it up and Amarina called her name three more times before she tapped Wylie.

"No more. Okay. You proved your point."

"So I did, didn't I?" Wylie grinned. "I'm glad you enjoyed yourself. Though I am sorry I woke you so early."

"Mm. No apology necessary," Amarina said.

"Good. Okay. I'm going to go get coffee. You coming?"

"Coming again? No." She laughed.

"Very funny," Wylie said.

They both got out of bed and Wylie poured them each a cup of coffee. She checked her watch. She still had plenty of time. She eased into a chair and took a sip.

"How's your leg?" Amarina asked.

"Sore, but manageable."

"Good. And Laurie will be back today so that'll take some of the pressure off you."

"Yeah. It's a good thing."

Wylie finished the week with no more incidents. She found another three pearls and managed to keep up the high shell count since Laurie wasn't completely up to speed.

On Saturday, she relaxed around the house and let her knee heal. She slept a lot, which wasn't like her, but she'd expended a lot of energy that week and figured she deserved it. When Amarina came home, they went out for dinner and spent a lovely night together.

The following morning, they lazed about the house until it was time to go over to Amarina's parent's house.

"Are you sure you're ready for this?" Amarina said.

"Sure. I loved your mum and dad. I can't wait to see them again."

"Good. I hope you like lamb. I didn't even ask."

"I love it. And I'm sure your mum knows her way around one."

"Yes, she does. You're in for a treat."

They drove the short distance to her parents' house. Wylie's knee was still sore, but she was able to maneuver much better. She managed the front steps with no problem, even though Mum had seen them coming and had sent Papa out to help her.

"I'm fine," she said. "But thank you."

"Heard what happened," he said. "That's a dangerous job you've got there, Wylie."

"It was my own carelessness," she said.

"Still. You can't be too careful down there."

"That's true."

The day was hot, but still they sat on the covered patio and Papa and Wylie drank beer while Amarina and Mum sipped homemade lemonade. The conversation was pleasant, between chatting about the hostel and pearl diving.

Papa asked Wylie about her hobbies.

"Do you like to fish?"

"I love it. I haven't had as much time to do it here as I'd like, though. I did go out one day and caught a nice five-and-a-half-foot tuna."

"What did you do with it?"

"Threw it back." She showed him the picture on her phone.

"He was a beauty. Would have made for some good barbecuing right there."

"At the time, I didn't know enough people to share it with. Now I realize I could bring it here and the family could get together and enjoy it."

"Well, how about we try again? I have a boat and plenty of gear. We could go out any night after work."

"How about tomorrow? That would be great."

"Great. I'll be waiting when you get off the diving boat."

The rest of the evening passed quickly, with Wylie drinking way more beers than she'd intended to. Or than she should have.

"You and my daughter are awfully tight," Papa said.

Wylie's gut clenched. Had he noticed? Had she been too obvious? She was paranoid that she had done something to out Amarina. She took a deep breath.

"I think everyone should have good friends."

"She's going to miss you when you leave."

"I'm sure we'll keep in touch," Wylie said.

"She doesn't usually get this close to someone staying at the hostel. And I don't really see that you two have anything in common."

"We're just really good friends. I can't speak to where it comes from, but it's there." Wylie hoped the explanation was satisfactory.

The evening came to an end and hugs were given all around. Papa patted Wylie on the back.

"See you tomorrow evening, then?"

"Definitely."

"Did you have fun?" Amarina asked on the way home.

"I did. I had a blast. But man, did I catch a buzz."

"I noticed," she laughed.

"I hope I didn't embarrass you."

"Not at all. I think my dad was a bit buzzed, too."

"Phew. I'm glad to hear that. I'm looking forward to fishing with him tomorrow."

"I wish I could go. But Mum and I will just have some more girl time while we wait for you to get home."

They got home and Wylie started to undress Amarina.

"When I get buzzed I get horny," she said.

"Lucky for me."

"Mm."

Wylie got her naked and then took off all her own clothes. She tried to pull Amarina to the couch, but Amarina insisted they go to the bedroom.

"I want all the room I can get to spread out with you and for you," she said.

"Works for me."

Wylie pulled her to her and kissed her hard on her mouth. She kissed her in such a way that all her passion showed in that one kiss. When the kiss ended, they were both breathless.

"Oh, my God," said Amarina. "That was some kiss."

"Yeah, it was. Consider it a prelude of what's to come."

She lay on the bed and pulled Amarina down with her. She kissed her again on the mouth. Then her cheek. Then her neck. She nibbled down and sucked where her neck met her shoulder. She kissed lower, down her chest to her heaving breasts. She took one with both hands and sucked hard on her nipple. She pulled it deep into her mouth and ran her tongue over it. She moved to the other breast and did the same. She loved the size and feel of Amarina's breasts and couldn't get enough of them.

But Amarina had other parts that Wylie loved as well and she wanted to make sure they got the attention they deserved. She continued to suck as she slid her hand down Amarina's body and ran it over her clit before plunging her fingers inside her.

"Oh God, yes," Amarina said. "Oh yes, Wylie."

Wylie thought to answer her, but didn't want to give up the hard treasure in her mouth. She continued to suckle Amarina while she thrust deeper inside her. Every time, she'd pull her fingers almost all the way out, then plunge them back in.

Amarina arched her hips in rhythm with Wylie. They moved together in their horizontal dance until Amarina cried out Wylie's name. She reached between her legs and held Wylie's wrist to hold Wylie's hand in place so she could come time and again.

"Oh, my God," she said when she could finally speak. "We need to get you drunk more often."

Wylie laughed.

"Not drunk. Just buzzed. And horny. But you keep me horny baby. I don't really need to be buzzed to want you."

"That's good to hear. And I didn't think you did."

Wylie rolled over to her back and folded her arms behind her head. She was feeling pretty darned good for taking Amarina over the edge as many times as she had. She closed her eyes and relaxed. But Amarina had other plans for her.

"You just get as comfy as you need to," she said. "Because I'm going to make you feel things you've never felt before."

"My, what happened to my shy insecure Amarina?"

"I want to sound bold. I'm not, though. You know that." She laughed.

She nibbled on Wylie's neck before kissing down to take one of her nipples in her mouth. She took half of Wylie's breast with it.

"I love how small and perfect your breasts are," Amarina said. They're not even a handful, but they're perfect for me."

She released the nipple and continued to kiss down her body until she arrived between her legs. She inhaled deeply the scent that was all Wylie. She lowered her mouth and ran her tongue over her.

"You taste so good," she said. "You're absolutely delicious."

Wylie reached down and ran her fingers through Amarina's hair. Amarina moved her tongue to Wylie's clit and licked and sucked it until Wylie came for her. Then she licked inside her, dragging her tongue along her inner walls, sticking her tongue as deep as she could go.

"Oh yeah," Wylie said. "That's it."

In no time Wylie was coming again, letting the tension flow out of her as the climax washed over her.

"You're amazing, baby," Wylie said when Amarina was in her arms.

"You know I don't really know what I'm doing."

"I beg to differ."

"All I do is enjoy myself and it makes you feel good."

"Well, whatever you're doing, you just keep on doing it."

Chapter Eighteen

The next day went great for Wylie. She got a lot of shells and found two more pearls. She worked hard, but felt good. And Laurie was definitely back to one hundred percent, which took the pressure off the other divers.

She was feeling good when she got off the boat and looked around for Papa. She heard him call her name and walked over to the boat. It was a nice looking boat, white with a blue stripe down it. It looked to be about twenty feet long with lots of rods sticking out from their holders. Wylie couldn't wait to get started.

"What are we fishing for?" she asked when she was onboard.

"Whatever you want. You want to catch another tuna?"

"I'd love to, but I don't know if I have the strength to reel it in after diving all day."

"Well, if you catch him, I'll help you land him. Between the two of us we should be good, right?"

"We'll see," Wylie said.

They set out for open water and Papa anchored the boat. He handed her a rod and asked if she wanted him to bait it for her.

"No, thanks. I can handle baiting my own line."

"Okay. Just checking."

They tossed their lines in and sat back. Papa came up to the front of the boat where Wylie was.

"Here," he said. "I brought beer."

"Thank you." Wylie sat up straight. "I really appreciate that."

She popped the top and took a long drink.

"That's good," she said. "Thanks again."

"No problem. I thought you'd enjoy one after a long day at work."

They sat there for an hour or so without a bite. Wylie had a couple more beers. She was feeling nice and relaxed.

"So no nibbles, huh?" Papa said.

"I've had a couple. Nothing serious."

"Speaking of serious," Papa said.

Wylie braced herself. She needed another beer. She grabbed one and braced herself for what was sure to come.

"How serious are you about Amarina?"

"How do you mean, sir?"

"Well, what's going to happen, Wylie? How do you see this whole thing playing out? I'm very curious."

"Curious about?"

"I don't know. It just seems your friendship is so intense. I'd like to know more about it."

"I'm not sure what to say, sir. She's a very dear friend. We've grown quite close in a short while."

"I'm not sure that's natural," he said.

"Natural, sir?"

"Natural, you know—"

He stopped mid-sentence when Wylie's pole bent in half. She picked it up and started the struggle with the fish. She fought long and hard and finally had to hand the pole to Papa for a turn. She was exhausted and felt like her arms would surely fall off. He fought the fish for another fifteen minutes and it was close to the boat.

Wylie took over and reeled the big tuna in while Papa grabbed the net. They finally landed it and both collapsed.

"This is huge," Papa said. "I'd like to keep it for a barbecue if I may?"

"Sure thing."

Papa chopped off its head and together they lifted it so the blood flowed over the edge of the boat and into the ocean. When most of the blood had drained, Papa turned to Wylie.

"Have you had enough for this evening or do you want to keep on fishing?"

"Oh, man. I'm wiped out. Let's call it a day."

"Sounds good. I'll pull up the anchor."

They made their way back to port and Wylie stayed with the boat while Papa got his truck. Together they got the tuna into the back of his truck.

"Do you want me to come over to help you get him out of the truck and get him cleaned?" Wylie said.

"No, thanks. I think I can handle it. I'll just drop you off at Amarina's."

When they got to Amarina's house, Papa put a hand on Wylie's arm.

"Look," he said. "You got lucky with that fish hitting when it did. I like you, Wylie. And Amarina clearly likes you. Don't make us change our minds."

"No, sir. I won't." Although she had no idea what she meant by that. She had no way of knowing how much he suspected and how obvious she was being.

Amarina greeted her at the door.

"How was it?"

"It was great. We caught a big ol' tuna. Your dad's gonna barbecue it. I'd imagine we'll be invited over this weekend. Everyone will be. That thing was huge."

"That's wonderful," Amarina said. She threw her arms around Wylie. "I'm so glad you had fun. Isn't my dad the greatest, too?"

"Yeah. I really like him. And he seems like me, too."

"Of course he does. What's not to like?"

"Aw. Thank you, baby."

"You may be wonderful and all, but man, do you stink. You need a shower."

"Yeah, I do," Wylie said. "I'll meet you in bed?"

"Sounds good."

Wylie stood there and let the water wash over her, taking away the stench of the day's activities. She looked down at her leg and remembered she was supposed to get her stitches out that day. Oh well, she'd do it tomorrow.

She dried off and climbed into bed with Amarina.

"How was your day?" she asked.

"It was nice. Mellow."

"Good. So your dad was asking questions about our friendship."

"Like what?"

"Like he thinks it's awfully intense and doesn't understand it because we have nothing in common."

"He'd never think I'm gay. I'm sure you're just being paranoid."

"I hope so."

Wylie snuggled closer and nuzzled Amarina's neck.

"What do you think you're doing?" Amarina said.

"What do *you* think I'm doing?"

"It feels good, but you've got to be exhausted."

"I am," Wylie said. "But you're so bloody hard to resist."

"Well, I'm not going to complain."

"Good."

Wylie loved her then. Slowly, patiently, as if she had all the time in the world. When her muscles ached, she pushed through the pain. Anything to please Amarina.

When Amarina was sated, she curled up in Wylie's arms and they fell asleep.

Wylie woke up the next morning starving since she hadn't had dinner the night before. She also had a bit of a headache from the beer she drank on her empty stomach. She poured herself some coffee and dug some leftovers out of the fridge. She was on her second cup of coffee when Amarina woke up.

"Hey, gorgeous," Wylie said.

"Good morning. How are you feeling this morning?"

"Like I've been rode hard and put away wet, but I'll survive. How are you?"

"Mm. I'm wonderful." She smiled.

"I'm glad. Hey, would you mind taking me to the doctor after work? I need to get these stitches out."

"I'll take them out for you."

"Say what?"

"No. Seriously. It's not a big deal. Here. Put your leg up on this chair."

Wylie did as she was instructed and watched as Amarina carefully removed the stitches from her knee.

"Wow. Do you have some kind of medical training?"

"No. Mum taught me. She never took us to the doctor to have stitches out. She always did it herself."

"Well, I learned something new about you today."

The rest of the week went by uneventfully, and it was Sunday again. Sure enough, the family had been invited to Mum and Papa's for tuna. Wylie was excited. She couldn't wait to taste her catch. Even though Papa had had to freeze it for a few days, she hoped it would be delicious. She was also nervous. She was determined not to be caught alone with either Steven or Papa. Which reminded her, she needed to text her boss and ask for another month off. She was sure they'd let her have it. She was a hard worker and they wouldn't let her go. It was really more of a courtesy thing. She promised herself she'd do it the next day.

Wylie fought the urge to hold tight to Amarina's hand when they walked to the backyard of her parents' house.

"Are you nervous?" Amarina asked.

"A little. But I'll be fine."

"Sure you will."

Mum saw them, rushed over, and gave them each a heartfelt hug.

"We're so glad you could make it," she said.

"We wouldn't have missed it," Wylie said.

"That was some fish you caught."

"Thanks. It was fun. I was just glad Papa was there to help me bring it in."

"He said you did most of the work," Mum said.

"It was definitely a group effort."

"Well, I'm sure it will taste good and that's really all that matters," Mum said.

Wylie and Amarina cut through the backyard to the ice chest. Amarina took a soda while Wylie grabbed a beer. They wandered back to the barbecue where several of Amarina's siblings and their spouses were gathered around Papa.

"Bloody good job catching this," Danny, the brother closest to Amarina's age, said.

"Thanks. He put up quite a fight."

"That's what Dad said."

"I was glad he was there to help me reel it in. My arms were so sore from diving that day."

"I bet. Well, good job."

"Thanks."

Wylie and Amarina stood in the crowd, mostly listening. Occasionally, someone would ask Wylie how diving was or Amarina how things were at the hostel, but for the most part, they just listened to the conversations playing out around them.

Finally, it was time for dinner. Mum brought the side dishes out and set them on a long table. Papa served the tuna. It was delicious. Wylie really hadn't doubted he'd know how to barbecue it. It had just the right amount of lime juice and hickory flavor. It was perfect.

"This is great," she told him.

"It's all on you." He patted her on the back. "We'll have to do it again sometime."

"Definitely."

He walked off and she finished her dinner. Amarina and Wylie said their good-byes and went home.

"So Dad wants to take you fishing again, huh?"

"Heck yeah. And I want to go. That was so much fun."

"I'm so glad you two get along. And that you have this in common. You should have set up a time to fish again, though. Instead of just saying you want to go."

"True. Maybe you can talk to him on Wednesday when you go over there? Or were you not planning on visiting them this week?"

"Oh, I have no problem visiting them. I love to see them."

"Great. I'm free any night after work that you won't mind."

"I never mind, silly. I love you and my dad hanging out together."

They settled onto the couch to watch some television, but soon Wylie became aware only of the nearness of Amarina. She could smell the fresh air on her skin and feel the warmth of her body. She stood in front of her, with one hand on either side of her shoulder.

"What are you doing? I can't see the television," Amarina said.

"I'm tired of the television," Wylie said. She lowered herself and took Amarina's lips with hers. They were soft and yielding.

"Wylie Boase, I swear you have a one-track mind."

"Guilty as charged. But can you blame me? Just look at you."

"I'm not much to look at, Wylie."

"Oh yes, you are. You underestimate yourself."

She kissed her again to forestall any further arguing. Amarina relaxed and let Wylie have her way with her. Wylie kissed her long and hard until she couldn't stand it anymore. She stood and took Amarina's hand. She led her once again to the bedroom where she stared lovingly at her.

"Do you have any idea how much you mean to me?" she asked.

"You're going to make me blush."

"I love it when you blush."

And true to form, a rich pink started at Amarina's chest and worked its way up her neck to her cheeks.

"Ah. There it is," Wylie said. She pulled Amarina close and let her bury her face in her chest. "You're so cute. I mean really. If you look cute up in the dictionary, you'd see your face."

"Oh my God. Now I'm blushing even more."

"Well, let's get you out of these clothes so I can show you how beautiful I think you are instead of just telling you."

They quickly stripped and climbed into bed. Wylie kissed Amarina passionately and moved her hand all over her body. She slid it between her legs and stroked her until Amarina screamed her name.

It was a frantic lovemaking session, but it had been what Wylie had needed. Quick and to the point. She felt much better as she drifted off to sleep.

The next morning, as she drank her first cup of coffee, she realized it was time to contact her boss again to ask for an extension of her stay in Australia. She was sure he'd say yes, but to make it official, she texted him. She hadn't figured with the time difference, it was noon in California. She got a text right back. It told her to feel free to take an extra month. It said she'd always have a job waiting for her when she got back. Now, the only issue was, could Wylie stay in the closet that long?

She sat staring at the phone while a knot developed in her gut.

"Hey, babe. You okay?" Amarina padded out to the kitchen.

"I'm good," Wylie said. "How are you this morning?"

"Mm. Someone took good care of me last night."

"Oh yeah. Well, good. I'm glad you enjoyed it."

"Wylie? Are you okay? You seem a million miles away."

"I'm fine, baby. I just heard from my bosses that I can stay. Now, join me for another cup of coffee?"

Chapter Nineteen

Wylie went through the motions the next few days. She got a decent number of shells each day and found a couple of pearls. But at home, she felt nervous and tight. She knew she had to talk to Amarina about coming out, but she didn't know how to start the conversation. She had no idea how to broach the subject. And she had no idea what Amarina would say or do.

Wednesday evening, on their way home from the pub, Amarina glanced over at Wylie.

"You want to tell me what's going on?" she said.

"What do you mean?"

"I mean you're distant, you're withdrawn. You haven't made love to me since Sunday. Something's up. Just tell me what it is."

"It's nothing," Wylie said.

"I don't believe you."

They got out of the car and went in the house. Amarina went to the fridge and grabbed a couple of beers. She handed one to Wylie. Amarina stayed in the kitchen to make dinner while Wylie leaned against the bar from the living room side.

Wylie took a long pull on her beer and thought hard about what to say to Amarina. She went about her business in the kitchen and stopped occasionally to look at Wylie. Wylie looked away each time.

Amarina served dinner and sat next to Wylie. She took her hand.

"Wylie, whatever it is, I can help you. You just need to tell me."

Wylie took a deep breath and steeled herself to tell Amarina what was going on.

"Baby. I don't even know how to say this."

"Just say it, babe. I'm here for you."

"I don't know how much longer I can go on pretending to be just your friend."

Amarina's hand went limp in Wylie's.

"I'm so sorry, baby. I care too much about you. I'm afraid I'm going to blow it for you."

Amarina pulled her hand away.

Wylie reached for her hand again, but Amarina was having nothing to do with it.

"Baby, please. I've been trying to figure out how to talk to you about this. As soon as I heard back from my boss that I could stay, it hit me that that meant another month of lies. I don't know how much longer I can do it."

"Really? You don't think you care enough about me to keep up the pretense?"

"You make it sound easier to do than it actually is."

"It is easy to do. We've done it so far."

"Not exactly. Your dad was in the middle of asking about us when the fish hit my line. I'm afraid to go out with him again, if you want to know the truth. I don't know how long I can keep lying to everyone."

"It's not that hard. I've been doing it most of my life."

"But I haven't. Don't you see? I've been out, loud, and proud since college. I hate being back in the closet and I don't know I can stay in it here. I'm so afraid I'm going to reach for your hand at your folks' house. Or that I'm going to screw up and call you baby."

"You won't. If you really care about me, you won't do it."

"But how can I be sure? I've come so close to doing it at the hostel. I just don't want to ruin your perfect life."

"Fuck you for patronizing me."

"I'm not. I'm just saying. You've got a job you love and you're close to your family. That's awesome. I don't want to ruin it."

Amarina silently shrunk down in her seat. A tear escaped her right eye and trickled down her cheek. Wylie took her hand. She did not protest.

"I suppose I should say I'm sorry," Amarina said. "I should apologize for making your life so difficult. But remember what your family did to you? I should think that you, of all people, would understand why I need to stay in the closet."

"But your relationship with your family is so different from the one I had with mine," Wylie said. "Your family loves you. I'm not sure mine ever did."

"Oh, don't give me that rubbish. How could they not have?"

"I just never fit in. Even as a kid. I was too much of a tomboy for my super feminine mother."

"Okay, so it was no great loss to you when they disowned you. That wouldn't be the case for me."

"How can you say it wasn't a big deal? Being disowned by a family is always hard. Just because I don't think they loved me. Well, obviously they didn't, but it doesn't mean I didn't feel abandoned."

"Fine. Then you *do* know how it feels. And you'd want that for me?"

"It's hardly that simple, Amarina."

"I think it is. You don't care how I feel as long as you can live openly."

"That's not what I'm saying. I'm saying I'm afraid I'm gonna blow it and I really don't want to."

"Maybe this is just your way of getting out of things," Amarina said.

"Getting out of things?"

"Yes. You can't live in the closet so you need to move home."

"Wait a minute. You're talking crazy now."

"Am I?" Amarina said. "I see it clearly now. I'm not crazy. This is your way of moving back to the States."

"It's not. It's simply my way of asking you to come out to your family. I'll be there with you. I think you can do it."

"I can't."

"You can't or you won't?" Wylie said.

"I would if I could, but I can't. I need my family."

"So where does that leave us?"

"Right where we are. I'm not going to come out to them. And you're going to go back home."

"But I don't want to."

"Sure you do," Amarina said.

"I don't. Why won't you listen to me? I want to stay with you. I'm just really afraid I'm going to out you."

"And if you care about me at all, that won't be an issue."

"I don't think you understand," Wylie said. "Being out is second nature for me. It takes a conscious effort for me not to acknowledge our relationship."

"I think you need to leave."

"Are you kicking me out?"

"Maybe I am. Maybe I have to."

"Amarina—"

"Look, you're threatening my relationship with my family. That's not something I'm going to sit back and take lightly."

"I'm sorry. I'm just being honest. I wanted you to know my fears."

"And now I know. You're afraid. But of what, really? Maybe being in a relationship is at the bottom of this."

"That's not true. I love being with you."

"Obviously, not enough. Get your things. I want you out."

"So, I go back to the States. Then what?"

"And then what happens?" Amarina said.

"Yeah. I haven't given up on us yet."

"So, what? We keep in touch by email? Social media? The occasional phone call? What the hell kind of relationship is that?"

"Baby, if that's the relationship we have to have, then we'll have to take it. I'm willing to try to make it work."

"Bullshit," Amarina said. "You'll be there alone and back to your womanizing ways."

"No, I won't. I don't want any other woman but you."

"You say that now."

"I'll say that later. Today, tomorrow, next week, next month. You're the only woman for me. You need to believe me."

"You know what? That's not going to work for me," Amarina said.

"What?"

"It's not going to work. I want you to leave my house and leave my life right now. Just get out."

"Baby, I don't want to just go. I don't want to leave things like this."

"You don't have a choice. I'm kicking you out. We're through. Get your things."

"Amarina," Wylie said. "You're not being reasonable."

"I am. I'm looking at things realistically. You're trying to paint some rosy picture for me that we both know won't even come close to the reality."

"I don't know that. I don't know why you won't believe me."

"Because I don't. Now, get your stuff. I'll take you wherever you want me to. Except my hostel. You're not welcome there."

Wylie grabbed her things and shoved them in her backpack. She carried it to the living room.

"Amarina, I wish you wouldn't do this."

"I don't have any choice. Why prolong the inevitable? Since you're leaving my life, I'd rather you do it now than later on."

"Okay. If this is how you want this to go down."

"This is your choice, Wylie. Not mine."

Wylie sighed. She fought back tears. She wanted to beg Amarina to let her stay, to help her come out to her family, to let her make love to her one more time. But Amarina's mind was made up. Wylie believed they could make a long distance relationship work. Obviously, Amarina didn't.

Wylie had Amarina drop her off at another hostel. Fortunately, there was a room there. She checked in and went to her room. She sat on her bed and buried her face in her hands. Things couldn't have gone more wrong. She'd truly believed Amarina would go for coming out to her family. They were so solid and her family loved her so much. And then, when she'd said no, Wylie had hoped she'd go for a long distance relationship. At least then, they'd still have each other. Wylie couldn't imagine the rest of her life without Amarina.

The next day on the boom, Wylie told her boss she'd only be able to work for another week. She lied and told them she'd just heard from her boss back home and she had to get back.

"That's too bad, Boase," the captain said. "You're a damned good diver. I'd love to see you stick around."

"Me, too. But I have responsibilities at home that I need to take care of."

"Oh, I understand. You're not the first backpacker to make a few bucks diving, then head home. It's okay."

Wylie finished work that day, then went back to her hostel and made her plane reservations for the following Friday. She couldn't believe she'd be leaving in a week. The idea of going back to California seemed surreal to her.

The next day after work, she went to the office of TSP to give her official notice.

"We're sorry to see you go," Nadine said. "Everyone really liked you."

"Thank you. I'm sorry to be leaving."

"If you ever find yourself in the area again, you'll always have a job with us."

"Thank you," Wylie said again. "I do hope to take you up on that."

She left the office feeling melancholy. She had a job if she ever came back. And she wanted to come back. But if she did, how would Amarina react? She couldn't worry about that. She just needed to focus on getting home now.

The next week flew by for Wylie. Soon, it was Friday and she was on the plane for her flight back to Brisbane. From there she flew to Los Angeles and from there, she took a small plane home. She took a taxi from the airport to her house and sat there, feeling like a stranger in her own home. She walked from room to room and checked things out. She made sure nothing had been disturbed in her time away.

She had no food in the house but was too exhausted to go shopping. Instead she climbed into bed and fell into a deep sleep. She woke up late Sunday afternoon and took a shower. She went grocery shopping for the basics and also picked up a six-pack of beer and a bottle of Scotch.

Wylie got home and opened a beer and fired up her barbecue. She grilled a steak and made a salad. Nothing seemed real. She felt like she was in a dream. She'd gotten so used to eating with Amarina. And her last week in Australia, she'd eaten at restaurants. It felt weird to eat by herself in her home. She missed Amarina.

She booted up her computer and checked her email. Nothing from Amarina. Just something from her boss, Bruce, welcoming her back and telling her that they were starting a new project at Fifth and Hazel and that she should be there at six the next morning.

She sent Amarina an email, just to let her know she'd gotten home safely. And to say she missed her and hoped to hear from her soon.

Lonely and sad, she went to bed.

Five o'clock came early, but she was happy to have something to do to pass the time. She loved her job and couldn't wait to get started on her new project. She met the crew at the site and accepted all the pats on the backs and welcome backs. She told them all she'd been a pearl diver and even told them the bad parts of the job until Bruce finally showed up and put them all to work.

They called it a day at three and all headed to the local watering hole for happy hour.

"So, what were the Aussie women like?" Joe asked.

Wylie thought long and hard how to answer. She could come off as the player they expected her to be. Or she could tell them about Amarina.

"They were wonderful," she said. "There was one in particular I fell pretty hard for."

"You? Fell for someone?" Bruce said.

"I did." Wylie pulled out her phone and showed a picture of Amarina to the group.

"She doesn't look like your type," Joe said.

"No? Maybe not, but she sure stole my heart."

"So what happens now that you're home? A long-distance relationship?"

"I'm hoping so. She said no, but I haven't given up. We had a bit of a falling out though before I left. She actually kicked me out."

"Kicked you out? As in you were staying with her?"

"Yep. I was shacking up with a sheila."

"Wow," Bruce said. "That's impressive for you."

"Yeah. I know. But she was something special."

"Well, now that you're home and free, you can get back to your old ways, right?" Joe said.

"We'll see," Wylie said. "We'll see."

"Well, don't look now," Joe said. "But here comes one of your regulars."

Wylie didn't look, but felt the soft breasts press into her arm.

"Hi, Wylie. When did you get back?"

Wylie turned.

"Hi, Maryanne. I got back Saturday."

"Well, welcome home. You up for a game of pool?"

Wylie was torn. For some reason, she felt guilty even talking to Maryanne. Then she reminded herself she was a free woman. And besides, what harm was there in a game of pool?

"Sure," she said. "Let's play."

They played a game that Wylie won. Bruce and Joe had quarters on the table, so Wylie played first Bruce, then Joe, and beat them both. Maryanne was up again. As she racked the balls, she made sure to bend over and afford Wylie a luscious view down her top. Wylie thought how sumptuous Maryanne's breasts were and how nice it would be to have a little company in her empty house.

"Time for shots!" Joe called.

They all gathered around him and shot tequila. The amber liquid felt good as it flowed down Wylie's throat. She bought another round as well as another pitcher for the group. They worked hard and drank harder. That's just the way they functioned.

After the next round of shots, Wylie and Maryanne went back to the pool table, which Wylie ran. Maryanne came over to her and leaned against her.

"Why don't you ever go easy on me?" she pouted.

"Where's the fun in that?"

Bruce and Joe suggested they play doubles against the women. Bruce and Joe won, since Maryanne wasn't really much of a pool player. They all went back and sat at the bar. Bruce said his good nights and left.

The more they drank, the more Maryanne came on to her. Wylie was trying to think of a polite way to extricate herself from the situation. Then she got a text message.

She pushed the button on her phone and saw her picture of Amarina. Her sweet Amarina. She read the text. It was from Bruce saying not to be at the site until six thirty. She duly noted that, but had to get out of there.

"It's time for me to go," she said.

"It's still early," Maryanne said. She placed her hand on Wylie's arm. It was warm and soft, just like the rest of her. "Stay a little longer."

"No. I'm still suffering from jetlag. I need to get home. I'll catch you guys tomorrow."

Chapter Twenty

The next morning at the site, Joe gave Wylie a hard time. "You've lost your touch with the ladies, Wylie."

"How do you figure?"

"Maryanne was all over you yesterday. She was so primed for you. And you left. You just left her there. Why didn't you take her home?"

"I wasn't in the mood," Wylie said.

"You're always in the mood."

"Not last night. I was still wiped from the flights home."

"Okay. As long as it doesn't become a regular thing. You get laid more than most of the guys on the crew. I'd be so disappointed if that changed."

"Hey, Joe?" Wylie said. "You're forgetting I had a girlfriend in Australia. An honest to God girlfriend. It's not so easy to just start messing around again after your heart's been busted wide open."

"Oh yeah. I suppose that's true. Still, I hope it doesn't last long. You're my hero, Boase."

Just then Bruce walked over with instructions for the day's work. Wylie was happy to have something more to think about than Amarina and Maryanne.

The morning flew by, and the crew gathered in the shade to eat their lunches. Wylie checked her phone. No email from Amarina. No text. No communication. Her stomach felt heavy. She wasn't sure she'd be able to eat her lunch.

"What's up, Boase?" Bruce said. "You look like you've lost your puppy."

"Nothing. Sorry."

"You feel okay? You've got to eat something to keep up with the work."

"Yeah. I'll be fine."

She took a bite of her sandwich. The first bite stuck in her throat, but once she got past it, she was able to eat the rest of her lunch.

They went back to work and worked until three thirty. At that point, Bruce called an end to the day.

"You ready for some brews?" Joe asked Wylie.

"I don't think so. I think I'm going to head home."

"Ah, come on. Just one pitcher."

"Okay. But that's it. You won't want me there longer than that anyway. I'm not in a very good mood, so I won't be very good company."

"You'll be fine. You need to loosen up. Beer will help."

They'd barely walked in when Maryanne was sitting next to Wylie.

"You know you left me high and dry last night," she said.

"Well, not really dry."

"Sorry about that, Maryanne. I'm just not ready to get back into the swing of things. I'm still somewhat in Australia. Maybe later."

"I'll wait as long as it takes, sugar. I know what it's like to have a roll with you, so I'll be as patient as need be."

"I don't know how long it'll be."

"I'll wait though. Hell, where am I going anyway? I'll be here."

Wylie excused herself and went home. She turned on the television and put her feet up. The TV didn't hold her interest, though and soon she let her mind drift to Maryanne. She was a beautiful woman in the classic sense. She had long dark hair and brown eyes with long lashes. Her figure was made to be loved, with large, supple breasts and curves in all the right places. She was tall and fit well in Wylie's arms. Wylie felt like she was a fool for not bringing her home. At least she'd have a way to pass the time that wasn't simply watching the boob tube.

But then she thought of Amarina. Amarina, who hadn't contacted her since she'd kicked her out of her house. Amarina who hated her now. And yet Amarina was still too fresh a wound in her heart for her to move on.

Not that Maryanne would be moving on, necessarily, Wylie argued with herself. Maryanne would simply be a warm body to enjoy. It wasn't like she was going to replace Amarina. She almost had herself convinced to go back to the bar to see if Maryanne was still there. Almost. Then she thought it would be cheating on Amarina. She couldn't explain it to herself. She didn't owe Amarina anything. But still, the thought of being untrue to her made her feel guilty as hell.

It didn't make sense, but there it was. She felt like she was being untrue to a woman who clearly hated her. She thought she ought to have her head examined.

To take her mind off things, she set her mind to making dinner. She'd found a new recipe for stroganoff that she wanted to try. It turned out really good. She was impressed with herself. She enjoyed it with a nice red wine. After dinner, she cleaned the kitchen and checked her watch. Seven thirty. Oh boy. It was only seven thirty and she had nothing left to do for the evening but think of Amarina.

She sent her another email, telling her how work was going and saying that she missed her. She asked her to please send her an email so Wylie would know she was okay.

Wylie flipped through the channels on her television set and came to a documentary on pearl diving in Australia. Why not, she thought. May as well watch something else that would keep that wound fresh and painful.

And it did. She missed the crew she dove with. She missed diving. She couldn't even deny missing the danger that went with the dives. She missed it all. She turned off the television and went to bed with thoughts of Australia floating in her mind.

She awoke in the middle of the night from a nightmare. A shark had attacked the crew on her boom. She'd been the only one to survive. It had felt so real. She got up and splashed cold water on her face. She climbed back into bed, but sleep escaped her. She was exhausted when she left for work that morning.

Bruce was already there when she arrived and she arrived before the rest of the crew.

"You're here early," she said to Bruce.

"I was just going over the plans. I just wanted to make sure these next steps get done correctly."

"Okay. Well, tell me what I need to do and I'll get started."

She got her instructions and set about laying the bricks for the day. She was careful not to interfere with the plumbers and electricians and even the concrete pourers. Bruce's crew worked foundation to finish, and Wylie was the only one who laid the bricks. She was damned good at it and was proud to see the job done. This one still had a lot of work to do on it, though. But she could see the finished building in her mind and knew it would look amazing.

She worked all day in the hot sun. They took a break for lunch around eleven-thirty. Wylie ate leftover stroganoff and drank iced tea and water. She was shooting the breeze with Joe and the others. She really enjoyed her crew. She liked what she did. And during the day, it kept her mind off Amarina. For the most part. If only her evenings were as easy to manage.

Bruce called it a day at a little after three.

"Last one to happy hour's a rotten egg," Joe said.

"I don't think I'm going," Wylie said.

"Man, you're really whipped, aren't you?" Bruce said.

"Whipped? Is that what you call it when she's dumped your ass?" Wylie said.

"I'm telling you," Joe said. "Take Maryanne home and let her help you forget about this Aussie chick."

Wylie thought about it. How could she possibly explain to the guys that she felt guilty? She supposed she could just say it and see what their reactions are.

"It's hard to explain," she said. "But I feel guilty even thinking about Maryanne."

"Oh yeah. You're whipped," Bruce said. "Whip whip."

"I suppose I am" Wylie said.

"You've got to get over her," Joe said. "Get back on the horse, so to speak."

"The horse, huh?" Wylie said.

"Sure. Take Maryanne for a ride." He laughed.

"The body is willing, but the mind says no," she said.

"Bummer for you. Hell, I'd take her for a spin if she swung my way."

"Well, she doesn't."

"Nope. And she wants you and you won't give her the time of day."

"At any rate," Wylie said. "I'm not going to happy hour today. Thanks, though. I'll see you guys tomorrow."

She couldn't stand the thought of being alone in her house another night. So she went to her favorite Mexican food restaurant. She ordered a Cadillac margarita and sat enjoying her chips and salsa as she waited for her meal. Her thoughts were interrupted by an unfamiliar voice.

"Wylie? Wylie Boase, is that you?"

Wylie stared up into the blue eyes that belonged to a nice looking blonde. But she had no idea who this woman was.

"It's me, Olivia Cramer. I lived next door to you in the dorms."

"Of course!" Wylie said. "I remember you."

"You look exactly the same," Olivia said.

Wylie couldn't say the same. Olivia had grown from a dumpy girl to a beautiful woman.

"You look great," Wylie said. "Really great. Care to join me?"

"I'll have a drink with you. For old time's sake. But I'm here with a group of friends."

Wylie signaled the waitress for two more margaritas.

"So, what do you do for a living?" Wylie asked.

"I'm a stewardess. And you?"

"I'm a bricklayer."

"Didn't you do that in college?"

"Yeah. And then I decided I wanted to stay in town so I just kept doing it. Are you still here in town?"

"No. Some friends and I just thought it would be fun to come up here for a few days. You know, get away from the families and just have fun. See old sights. Check out the old haunts. Do you still go to The Oasis?"

"Every day pretty much." Wylie laughed. "So, not much has changed for me."

"How fun. So, Wylie, tell me, are you seeing anyone?"

"Nope. Not at the moment."

"You never were a one-woman woman, as I recall."

"Yeah. Monogamy has never been my strong suit. And you? Anyone in your life?"

"I have a wonderful wife and we have two little girls."

"Congratulations."

"Thanks."

Wylie's dinner arrived and Olivia rose to leave.

"It was really great seeing you, Wylie. You take care of yourself."

"You, too."

Wylie ate her dinner with a smile on her face as she allowed her mind to take a trip down memory lane to the great times they'd had in the dorms. Half the eighth floor had been lesbians. They'd had so much fun. Wylie had slept with most of them. But never Olivia. Olivia had always been a sweetheart. Naïve and sweet and Wylie had been afraid to hurt her. But damn if she wouldn't mind spending some time with her now. But she was all grown up and married with kids. Wylie thought how nice it would be to settle down. To have someone to miss her if she ever went away with friends. To have someone waiting for her at home when she got off work. To have Amarina, she thought. That's what she wanted. Amarina.

The next day, she got to work early and waited until Bruce got there.

"Hey, Bruce, can I talk to you?"

"Sure. What's up?"

"I need to go back to Australia."

"Wylie, you need to really think hard about this. Look, I get you're hurting, but to go all the way back there for some chick who kicked you to the curb? Do you really think that's a good reason to go there?"

"I have to try, Bruce. I have to try to make it work with her."

"When? Like tomorrow? Next week? What are you talking, Wylie?"

"I don't know. I'm not sure when I'll get there. I have things to take care of first, obviously. But I have to go back. I want to keep working for you until that time and I'll give you plenty of notice when I know when I'll be leaving. But I wanted to be upfront with you now. I need to go back. Sooner rather than later."

"Well, if that's the way it has to be, then so be it. Just keep me posted. Until you give me notice, I'll just treat you like any other employee."

"Fair enough. And, Bruce?"

"Yeah?"

"Thanks."

After work, Wylie logged on the computer to see about applying for a longer visa. There were several options to choose from. She longed to click on the skilled work visa to live and work in Australia permanently, but she had to be realistic. She didn't know how long she'd want to stay if Amarina really wouldn't take her back. But she believed she would. She had to. She needed Amarina and figured she had to be as miserable without Wylie as Wylie was without her.

So she opted for a working holiday visa until she saw that she was too old. In the end, she chose the same, regular three-month visa and decided to see what would happen when the visa ran out. Hopefully, she'd be able to extend her stay, but that was a worry for the future. For now, she just needed to get back to Amarina. If it turned out she couldn't extend her stay and Amarina wouldn't go back to the states with her…Well, she refused to think about that now.

She was so close to getting to Australia, she could smell the salt water and feel the humid air.

She sent Amarina an email letting her know she was coming back. She had a few more things to take care of, but she planned to be there soon and would she at least be able to see Amarina?

The next order of business for Wylie was TSP. She sent them an email letting them know she hoped to be back within a couple of months and would it be possible for her to get her job back? She received an email back saying they would love to have her back and for her to just come by the office when she got back to town and they'd get her set up.

Things were looking up. She spent her days hard at work and her nights preparing to go back to Broome. She still hadn't heard from Amarina and she almost stopped working toward getting back there, but deep down inside she believed Amarina really cared for her and would take her back once she showed that she was willing to do anything to be with her, including keeping their relationship a secret.

Wylie found a nice couple who wanted to rent her house. They were young and childless, though they couldn't promise to stay that way for long. They loved her house, the location, everything about it. They set up a payment system and Wylie told them they could move in in two weeks.

So, a month after she started planning her journey back to Broome, she was ready to go. She gave Bruce two weeks' notice and continued to do her job every day. She continued to email Amarina every night, but still didn't hear from her. She wondered anew if she was throwing her life away for nothing.

"It's your last day at work," Joe said. "Come to happy hour with us."

"Okay," she said. "Why not? One last time."

The whole crew went. They were rowdy and fun-loving and everyone wanted to buy Wylie a shot and toast her to wish her well. She played pool and drank beer and tequila and had a great time.

Maryanne wasn't there, but another of Wylie's paramours was. Her name was Gail, and she was a looker, to be sure. Wylie was well aware of Gail watching her. She finally crossed the bar and came to Wylie's side.

"Long time no see," she said.

"No, I haven't been here for a while."

"What's the occasion? Seems like a party."

"I'm going to Australia tomorrow. So they're throwing me a good-bye party."

"Oh yeah? How long will you be gone?"

"Hopefully forever," Wylie said.

"Forever? That's an awfully long time."

"Yeah. Well, that's what I'm hoping for. We'll see if it works out."

"Well, why don't you and I get out of here and make some memories this last night of yours?"

"Tempting though that may be, I have to get up early in the morning, so no fun and games for me tonight," Wylie said.

"Oh, come on. I've never known you to turn down a good time."

"I'm sorry, Gail. Trust me. I'd love to take you home. But I just can't. It's about time for me to head out anyway. You take care of yourself, okay?"

Wylie said good-bye to the gang and headed home. She needed to get some shut-eye before she started the next phase of her life.

CHAPTER TWENTY-ONE

Two days later, Wylie climbed on a small plane in Perth that would take her to Broome. She was exhausted, excited, and nervous all at once. She sat in her seat and stared out the window, the familiar sights causing her to be nostalgic.

As the plane flew over the familiar red dirt as they got closer to Broome, Wylie's heart beat faster. She thought it would burst out of her chest. She was really doing this. She had really turned her back on her life back home to have a chance with Amarina. But what if Amarina had moved on? What if she had found someone new and fallen in love with them?

No, she wouldn't have done that. She couldn't have. She had to know Wylie was the only woman for her. After all the good times they'd had together, surely she knew that.

The plane touched down at the tiny Broome airport. Wylie's heart was in her throat. She walked over to the car rental booth and picked up the car she'd reserved. She didn't know how long she'd need it, but she'd rented it for a week.

Next stop was the hostel where she'd reserved a room. It wasn't as nice as the one Amarina ran, but it was a room to sleep in, anyway. She parked her car around back and let herself into her room. It was pretty basic, as was to be expected. She sat on the bed and took a deep breath, steeling herself for what was to come next. She had no idea how Amarina would respond to seeing her. She'd sent her email after email so she knew she should be there today. Still, how would she react to seeing her?

She heaved herself off the bed, let herself out, and started down the street. It was four thirty. Amarina should be working until five. She should get there with plenty of time to spare.

She arrived at the hostel and looked through the window. She could see Amarina sitting at the desk. She took a deep breath and walked in the door. Amarina looked up from her work. Wylie would have sworn for a brief second she looked excited before her face returned to neutral.

"Hey," Wylie said.

"Hello."

"How ya doin'?"

"I'm fine. Why are you here?"

"Did you get my emails?"

"I did."

Wylie felt the tension creep over her whole body. This was not going well. Not at all.

"So you knew I'd be back," she said.

"I didn't know for sure."

"I said I would."

"Still."

"I've always been honest with you, Amarina. You've never had to doubt my word. Ever."

"You haven't answered my question. Why are you here?"

"I want another chance, Amarina. I've missed you big time, and I want another chance with you."

"I don't know if I can do that," Amarina said.

Wylie felt her heart drop to her stomach. She needed Amarina to see how perfect they were together. She needed her to understand they belonged together.

"Please, baby. Just give me a chance."

Amarina's replacement arrived, and she gave him a rundown of what had happened that day. She grabbed her purse and came around to the lobby. Wylie took this as a good sign. She could have left through the back door. Wylie took in her plump figure dressed in a bright striped skirt and a neon yellow blouse. She looked fantastic.

"This is not the place for this conversation," Amarina said.

"Fine. Let me take you to dinner. Just dinner. We'll talk. Like adults," she added.

"Okay. Where to?"

Wylie led the way down the street to her favorite oceanfront restaurant.

"I should have known you'd choose this place," Amarina said.

"Of course." Wylie smiled. "I'm predictable."

They were seated and had placed their orders when Wylie took Amarina's hands.

"I've missed you so much."

Amarina pulled her hands away.

"I'm not sure you understand."

"Understand what?"

Amarina looked around the room then down into her lap before looking at Wylie.

"You broke my heart."

"I get that. I broke mine, too."

"I don't think you get it."

"Baby, I was miserable without you. I emailed you every day, didn't I?"

"I think that was to clear your conscience," Amarina said.

"No. It was because I missed you and wanted contact with you. And then when I didn't hear from you, I got worried. I started thinking something might have happened to you."

"How could I have answered your emails? What would I have said?"

"That you were fine. That you missed me. Anything. It just would have been nice to hear from you," Wylie said.

"If I would have answered, it would have been leading you on."

The waiter brought their food and Wylie took a deep breath and tried not to show her frustration.

"How is letting me know you're okay leading me on?"

"It would have been. Anything you heard from me would have given you false hope."

"Okay. So you say. It doesn't matter now," Wylie said. "I'm not emailing you right now. I'm sitting here in front of you, eating dinner with you. So, what do you say? Can we start over? Can we start seeing each other again?"

"I know what you're asking."

"Good. And?"

"You want to know if you can sleep with me."

Wylie sat back against the back of the booth. She felt like she'd been punched in the gut. Was Amarina hearing anything she said?

"Baby, listen to me. I got a room at a hostel. I'm willing to take this as slowly as you want. But I want to see you. I want to at least be able to take you to dinner. Or walk with you along the beach. I'm not in any hurry. Just tell me I can be in your life again."

"So you're telling me you'd be okay just being friends?"

Wylie thought long and hard before answering. She wanted to be so much more than friends with Amarina. But would it be worth it to tell her that? Should she say okay to friendship and then keep working for something more?

"I'm telling you I just want to spend time with you. If it's as friends, then so be it."

"You're lying," Amarina said. "You don't want to just be my friend."

"You're right. I want to be more than friends, but I'll take friendship if that's all you're willing to give."

"So, how long do you plan to stay this time?"

"Indefinitely."

"What does that mean? Until you chicken out again?"

"No," Wylie said. "I quit my job. I no longer need to go back for that. And I rented out my house, so I have nowhere to live there, either."

"Are you serious?"

"I am. Very. I want things to work between us, Amarina. I'm here for the duration."

"Wow." Amarina's cool demeanor seemed to melt somewhat.

"So, what do you say?"

"I still say you hurt me and have a lot of nerve showing up here expecting me to forgive you and say okay everything's fine."

"I'm not asking you to say everything's fine and that we can go back to how we were before. Not yet, anyway. But I still care very deeply for you and I have a hard time believing you could turn off your feelings just like that, either."

"You left. You *left*. My feelings are of no concern to you anymore. Don't you get that?"

"But they are. I can't turn mine off the way you apparently can. And I left because you kicked me out. Or don't you remember?"

Amarina said nothing.

"Look," Wylie said. "Let's start by being friends. Is tomorrow still your day off?"

"Yes."

"Let's go for a hike. What do you say?"

"Okay. A hike. But no hanky-panky."

"No. Amarina, I'll just be happy to spend time with you. I've missed you so much."

"What time?"

"I should swing by TSP and let them know I'm here and can start Monday, so any time after that. What about ten?"

"Ten sounds good. We'll meet at the Breakfast Nook down on the corner."

"Sounds great. I can't wait."

They walked out of the restaurant and stood in the parking lot. Wylie didn't want the evening to end.

"Where are you staying?" Amarina said.

"At the hostel just down the street from yours."

"Okay. So, it's not far. You don't need a ride."

It was more a statement than a question, but Wylie answered anyway.

"No. I don't need a ride."

They arrived at Amarina's hostel.

"Okay then. I'll see you tomorrow at ten."

"Definitely," Wylie said. "Have a good night."

Amarina got in her car and drove off.

Wylie had a smile on her face and a lightness to her step as she walked to her hostel. Spending a day with Amarina was almost more than she'd hoped for. She'd hoped to ease back into her life slowly, but she was going to get to spend a whole day with her, and she just wanted to shout it to the world.

The next morning, Wylie walked down the street to the offices of TSP. Nadine came around from her desk and gave Wylie a big hug.

"It's so good to see you again. I can't believe you came back so soon. I thought maybe we'd see you next year."

"No. I couldn't stay away. So, I'm back. I was wondering if I could start on Monday."

"Let me see if Ronald can see you now. You know, to fill out the paperwork and all that."

Wylie waited and Nadine came right back out.

"He'll see you now."

Wylie walked into Ronald's office. He stood and they shook hands.

"Wylie. It's so good to see you again. I was happy to hear you may be coming back. You were one of our best divers, even in the short time you were here, you showed a lot of potential."

"Thank you, sir. I can't wait to get in the water and start doing it all again."

"You'll have to go through orientation again, though I don't suppose that'll be a problem for you. So, here. These are the papers I've filled out. Sign here and here."

He pointed with his pen and Wylie signed.

"So, that's it? I'm good to go? I can start Monday?"

"Monday it is. I'll let the captains know."

"Thanks again, Ronald. I really do appreciate this."

"It's our pleasure, Wylie. Honest."

They shook hands again and Wylie left the office. She waved to Nadine and went out into the warm morning air. She checked her watch. It was nine thirty. So, she'd be early. So, what? She had nothing better to do, so she walked down to the Breakfast Nook. She took a corner table and sipped coffee until Amarina got there.

She stood as she saw her walk in. She took in her shoulder length mussed hair, her red shorts and pink blouse. She looked beautiful. Wylie fought the urge to meet her at the door and greet her with a hug and a kiss. Instead, she simply stood where she was.

"You look wonderful," Wylie said when Amarina had reached their table.

"Thank you."

They sat and Amarina picked up her menu, but Wylie couldn't stop staring at her. Amarina finally lowered her menu.

"Were you going to have something to eat?"

"Yeah. Sorry. I just can't get over how beautiful you are."

"Smooth talking isn't going to help you. Just so you know. I'm willing to see if we can spend a day together as friends. You're already being smooth. I'm telling you it's not going to help you get into my bed."

"No," Wylie said. "That's not what I'm doing. I just...I mean... it's just that I guess I'd forgotten how pretty you really are."

"Well, thank you, then. I appreciate it. Now, can we order?"

"Huh? Oh yeah. Of course."

The waiter came by and took their orders.

"So, did you go by TSP this morning?" Amarina asked.

"I sure did. I start Monday. They seem pretty excited to have me back."

"That's gotta feel good."

"It does. I can't wait to get back in the water. I bought a new wetsuit, too, so I won't have tears in it now."

"Smart move. I do hope you'll be careful down there."

She hoped Wylie'd be careful, huh? So, did that mean she really did care? Was she worried about her? Wylie decided to let it go at the moment, but she filed it away hopefully for use at a later time.

"I will. I don't need any more stitches."

"No, you don't."

They finished their breakfast and wandered out to the parking lot.

"Do you want to leave your car here or at the hostel?" Wylie said.

"I was thinking I'd drive us partway, then we can hike."

"That sounds great. Did you remember your suit under your clothes?"

"I did," Amarina said.

"Excellent."

They drove in silence until Amarina found a place to pull off the road and park. They'd passed very few hikers on their way, which made Wylie happy. She didn't want to share Amarina with anyone.

Wylie took in the red dirt and deep gorges and felt like she was truly home. She knew it didn't make sense. She'd only been there a month or so before, but it felt like home to her. She felt like she was where she belonged. And she felt like Amarina was who she belonged with. If only she could convince her.

They hiked for a couple of hours and then climbed down to the river. The shed their clothes and climbed into the cool, blue water.

"Oh, my God. This feels amazing," Wylie said.

"It really does. Especially after that hot hike. This is delicious."

Wylie swam up next to Amarina.

"I'm really enjoying today."

"So am I. But that doesn't mean anything's changed."

"But could it mean it might?" Wylie said.

"I don't know, Wylie. You've got me in a turmoil. It is wonderful to see you. I will admit that. But you hurt me and I'm not sure I'm willing to chance that again. Plus there's still the issue of my family."

"Baby," Wylie said. "I'm not going anywhere. You've got to believe me. And I've given it a lot of thought. It will take some effort, but I won't out you to your family. I swear."

"Look. You said you were willing to be my friend. And already you're pushing for more. Maybe we need to not see each other at all."

"No. I'm sorry. I'll cool my jets. It's just that spending time with you brings back all those memories."

"Well then, maybe we shouldn't spend time together."

"That's not what I'm saying," Wylie said. "I want to spend time with you. But please, give me some time to get used to your being just my friend, okay? I'd appreciate that."

"I suppose that's fair. Although it seems pretty twisted to me. We should start out as friends and see where it goes. Not start out as more, which is what you seem to want to do."

They got out of the water and were laying in the sun, drying off when Amarina's phone rang.

Wylie could only hear Amarina's side of the conversation.

"Hi, Mum…I'm sorry. I forgot…Wylie's back in town…no… we're in the gorge today…I don't know. I'll ask and let you know… okay. Good-bye."

"Everything okay?" Wylie said.

"Yes. I was supposed to spend the day with my mum, but I forgot."

Wylie smiled inwardly. So, she'd made Amarina forget about spending time with her mom, huh? That boded well for Wylie.

"I'm sorry," she said. "I feel bad now."

"No, don't. And she's all excited that you're back."

"Really? Well, at least someone is."

"She wants you to come to the family barbecue on Sunday."

Wylie felt the knot form in her stomach. The whole family would be there. She knew she didn't want to see Steven and Papa. They were the suspicious ones. She'd have to be on her best behavior.

"I don't know, Amarina…"

"I think it would be a good move for you, but it's your choice."

Shit, Wylie thought. Could she really face them right now?

CHAPTER TWENTY-TWO

The next few days, Wylie spent getting reacquainted with the town. She hung out at the beach a couple of days and went fishing one day, where she came up with absolutely nothing. She hoped that wasn't an indicator of things to come.

She stopped by the hostel every day to see Amarina, who agreed to go to dinner with her every night. They were at dinner Saturday night when Amarina broached the subject.

"So," she said, "you never told me whether or not you'd be willing to come over for the barbecue tomorrow. Mum's asked every time I've spoken to her."

Wylie felt nauseous. She didn't want to go. But if she said no, it could ruin her chances with the family, and therefore Amarina, forever.

"Sure, I'll go," she heard herself say.

"That'll be great. I'm sure Mum will be happy to see you again."

"It'll be awesome to see her, too. And the rest of your family."

Wylie was somewhat telling the truth. She was looking forward to seeing Mum. She'd missed her. But the rest of them? Who knew how they'd feel about her reappearing?

"So, can I get a ride with you? Or do I have to drive over there myself?" Wylie said.

"I'll pick you up," Amarina said. "You should probably be ready by noon."

"I can do that," she said. "This is going to be so much fun."

"I hope so," Amarina said. "Do I need to be worried about you breaking down my closet doors?"

"No. I promise. I'll be extra careful. I don't want to do anything you don't want me to do."

"I guess we'll find out if you can really do that."

Wylie wished Amarina would throw her a bone. Just a little bone would be nice. But she didn't. She was playing her hand close to the vest, and it was driving Wylie crazy. Wylie had to figure that going out every night had to mean something more than just friends. And inviting her to her parents' house had to mean something somewhat intimate, too, right? She didn't know. And she was getting so tired trying to read Amarina to figure out when she'd been given the green light to attempt to be more than friends.

Frustrating though it was, Wylie wasn't going to give up. She would persevere. She was crazy about Amarina. She just needed Amarina to believe it.

Wylie was waiting outside when Amarina pulled up the next day. It felt good to see Amarina in her car, and it was a nice familiar feeling to be in the car again.

"How are you today?" Wylie said.

"I'm fine. And you?"

"I'm great. A little nervous, but I'll be okay."

"I found out from Mum that Steven won't be there. That should make you feel better."

"Right. But there's still your dad."

"Right. There's still him."

That did nothing to soothe Wylie's nerves.

"You don't have to say it like that," Wylie said.

"You told me he was asking about us before."

"He was. He would have point-blank asked if we were lovers if that fish hadn't hit when it did. I'm telling you. So just don't leave me alone with him today and we should be good."

"Okay. I'll try to keep you two apart. I can't have you outing me, Wylie. I really can't."

They arrived at the house and Wylie took a deep breath.

"You going to be okay?" Amarina said.

"Yeah. Sure. Just preparing myself."

They walked into the backyard, and Mum came running down the back steps, arms up and apron swinging back and forth, to greet them.

"Oh my word," she said. "It's really true. You came back."

"Yes, ma'am, I did. I'm here for good."

"Well, isn't this something? Come on, let's get you a drink."

They left Amarina standing there as she led Wylie to the ice chest.

"I like you, Wylie Boase," Mum said. "I don't understand things. Amarina's never been this friendly with one of her clients before. But she really got attached to you, and it hurt when you just up and left. Let's see that that doesn't happen again."

"No, ma'am. That won't happen."

"Good. Because if it does, you'll never be welcome here again."

Wylie felt like she'd just been slapped in the face. The one person she'd hoped would be on her side was Mum. And now… Well, it really didn't matter because Wylie wasn't going anywhere.

"That will never happen, Mum. I'm here permanently now."

"Good. Let's go make the rounds."

Wylie had seen all Amarina's brothers and sisters and was standing with an empty beer bottle when she felt a gaze on her. She turned to find Papa staring at her. She walked over to the ice chest and grabbed a beer for herself and one for him. She swallowed hard. It was time to get this over with.

"Hello, Papa." She handed him a beer.

"Hello." He took the beer and clinked it against hers. "Thanks."

"You're welcome. How have you been?"

"Overall, pretty good. But it's been hard watching my youngest suffer like she has been. You weren't right to just up and leave. You know that."

"Yes, sir. I can see that. But it won't happen again."

"So, you ready to tell me what your intentions with Amarina are now?"

"Amarina is my dearest friend, sir. We had a falling out, and I ran instead of sticking around to work it out. It was immature of me, and it won't happen again. I've already spoken to TSP and have a job starting tomorrow."

"TSP?"

"The diving company."

"So, what about your responsibilities in the States? Surely they're calling to you? I'm sure you'll have to go back sometime, but I'd like it if you'd give Amarina a little more notice next time."

"I'm telling you I quit," Wylie said. "I quit my job and rented out my house. I have nothing left for me there."

"What about your family?" Papa said.

"I don't have any family," Wylie said.

"So you mean to tell me you're really here to stay this time?"

"Yes, sir. That's what I mean to tell you."

She was surprised when he wrapped his arms around her and pulled her into a tight bear hug.

"Wow," she said. "If only Amarina would welcome me back that enthusiastically."

"She'll come around. Don't tell her I know this, but she carried quite a torch for you, you know," Papa said.

"You wouldn't know it from how she's treating me now."

"It takes a while to trust again. Give her time."

"That's all I can do, sir. Let her know I'm here and wait until she decides she's ready."

"See? I knew you were a smart one, Wylie. Now, grab a plate. Food's ready."

Wylie wandered through the crowd until she found Amarina.

"Hey, your dad says food's ready. Come on. Let's get some."

"You sure were talking to him for a long time," Amarina said as they stood in line. "I thought you were going to avoid him."

"Yeah. He grilled me. As was expected. And chewed me out for hurting you. Again. Expected. It was a good talk, though."

"Good. I'm glad you two have bonded again. I wasn't sure that was possible. What do you mean he chewed you out for hurting me? How did he mean that?"

"That's a conversation you'll have to have with him. I think he just needed to understand that I really am back for good. And once he did, we were golden."

"So, you've got everyone convinced but me, huh?" Amarina said.

"I guess."

They filled their plates with food and sat at the long table with her siblings.

The conversation was light with everyone smiling and contributing. Everyone except Amarina. After dinner, Wylie went up to thank Mum and Papa for inviting her and found Amarina waiting by the car.

"Is something wrong?" Wylie said. "You hardly said a word during dinner and then you left without saying good-bye to your folks."

Amarina stood there, leaning against her car. Wylie saw a tear trickle down her cheek. Then another. Soon, Amarina was sobbing.

"Do you think this is easy? Do you think it's easy for me, Wylie?"

Wylie stood torn. Should she take her in her arms and hold her? Was she allowed? Did she just have to stand there? She shoved her hands in her pockets.

"What? Do I think what's easy?"

"You! Being with you all the time. Do you think it's easy?"

"I don't understand. I thought we were doing okay. You know, taking it slow, working our way to friendship."

"But it's not easy," Amarina said again. "I had some hard-core feelings for you, and now acting like I don't is killing me."

Wylie was silent for a moment as she let the words soak in. So, Amarina did still have feelings for her. She wanted to jump up and down. But instead she had to think what her next move should be. She took a step toward Amarina. She didn't stiffen. That was a good sign.

"Baby, then why do we act like this? I'm crazy about you. That never changed. I'm willing to be as patient as you need me to be, but it sounds like being patient isn't what you want."

"I don't know what I want. I just want you. But I want to know you're not going anywhere. I don't even care about my family knowing about us. I just know I want you with me forever."

"I'm with you, baby. I told you, I'm here to stay. And I've never lied to you before."

"That's true. You never have. But you've hurt me, Wylie. And I can't go through that kind of pain again."

"Do you understand that I've never felt the way I feel about you with anyone, ever, in my life? I gave up my life in the States to move here to be with you. I'm not going anywhere, baby. Trust me."

Amarina's crying had turned to dry sobs.

"So, you really care about me?"

"Baby, I love you."

"And you're not leaving?"

"No."

"Oh, Wylie." She threw her arms around her shoulders. "I love you, too."

Wylie held her tight, pressing their bodies together until she could wait no longer. She stepped back and tilted Amarina's chin up. She looked into her eyes and saw the love shining there. She lowered her mouth and took Amarina's with it.

The kiss was soft and tender at first, but soon Amarina opened her mouth and Wylie allowed her tongue to wander in. The kiss was intense and purposeful. Wylie made sure to let Amarina know every last thing she was feeling with that kiss.

When the kiss ended, they were both breathless.

"God I've missed you, Wylie."

"I've missed you, too, baby." They held each other for a moment or two, then Wylie said, "So, what's next? Where do we go from here?"

"You get in my car and we go back to my place right now."

"Sounds good to me."

She climbed in the car and sat there, throbbing, as she waited for the interminable ride to end. It was only a few blocks, but it seemed to be taking so much longer. All she wanted was to get home and ravish Amarina.

They finally arrived at Amarina's house, and Wylie scrambled out of the car. She went around to Amarina's side and held the door open for her. She helped her out of the car then pressed her back against the door and kissed her again. There was nothing soft or tender about that kiss. It was powerful.

"I'm sorry," Wylie said. "Did I bruise your lips?"

"I don't know and I don't care. Kiss me like that again."

Wylie was happy to oblige. When they came up for air, Amarina took Wylie's hand and led her to the front door. She turned to face her.

"I'm letting you back in," she said.

"I know."

"If you ever hurt me again, you will never be allowed back. Ever."

"I understand."

"Good."

She opened the door, and as soon as Wylie was in, closed the door behind them. She pressed Wylie into the door and kissed her. Wylie returned the kiss with all she had. She ran her hands up and down Amarina's sides while they kissed.

"Oh my God, I need you, Amarina," Wylie said.

"I need you, too, Wylie. But all in good time."

Wylie didn't know how much longer she'd be able to wait, but reasoned she'd wait as long as Amarina said to. She was close to being home free now and wasn't about to do anything to screw that up. If Amarina wanted to take it slow, then so be it.

"Go sit on the couch," Amarina said. Wylie did as she was instructed. Amarina went to the kitchen and returned with a couple of beers.

Wylie took hers and drank from it. It did little to cool the heat that had engulfed her body. She was burning for Amarina and Amarina was the only thing that could quench her thirst. She set her beer on the coffee table and turned to face Amarina.

"Baby, how long are you going to make me wait?"

"Just a little while longer. I want to relax with you. I want to enjoy a beer with you. I want to draw out the inevitable until neither of us can take it any longer."

"I don't know how much longer I can take it as it is," Wylie said.

"We'll see. Don't worry. I won't make it too long."

"Thank God."

"Now finish your beer, babe."

Wylie picked up her beer and took another long pull of it. It was nice and cool, and she allowed herself to enjoy it knowing that having Amarina was going to happen.

Soon they were both through with their beers.

"So, do we need more beer?" Wylie asked.

"I don't," Amarina said.

"Neither do I." She moved closer. She placed her hand behind Amarina's head and pulled her to her. She kissed her then, a passionate, love filled kiss. And Amarina returned the passion and the love. The kiss made Wylie's toes curl.

"I need to take you to bed," she said.

"Then take me, Wylie. Take me to bed and have your way with me."

Wylie stood and took Amarina's hand. Together, they walked to the bedroom, where Wylie went to work undressing Amarina. She slowly unbuttoned her blouse, driving herself crazy as she did. She wanted to rip her clothes off her. She couldn't wait to feel her skin touching her own. She longed to take a breast in her mouth and suckle it.

But she wanted to make the moment last. She wanted this to be special for both of them. She wanted this time to be something they'd never forget.

When she had Amarina's shirt off, she unhooked her bra and tossed it to the floor. She stood and stared into Amarina's eyes as Amarina took off her shirt and undershirt, leaving them both bare-chested. Wylie pulled Amarina to her and drew in her breath as their skin touched.

"Oh, my God, you feel so good," Wylie said. She bent over and wrapped her hands around one breast and took Amarina's nipple in her mouth. It was Amarina's turn to gasp. She grabbed Wylie's head and held it in place.

Wylie sucked hard at the nub and ran her tongue all over it. She loved how responsive Amarina was. She had missed her so much. She wanted her to know that. And she wanted to show her as only she could.

"Wylie, please. Oh God, that feels good. But I'm going to come."

"Come for me, baby. I need you to come for me."

"I can't standing up."

"Sure you can. I'll hold you up."

"No, please."

"Okay," Wylie said. "Sit on the bed."

Amarina sat and Wylie knelt in front of her and took her breast in her mouth again. She flicked her tongue over her nipple one more time, and Amarina cried out as she clenched Wylie's head to her chest.

"Oh dear God," she said. "Oh God, Wylie."

Wylie was not to be deterred. She unbuttoned Amarina's shorts.

"You know I'm just getting warmed up, don't you?" Wylie said.

"I know."

"So maybe you should pace yourself."

"Maybe I'll come every which way to Sunday."

"I'd like that," Wylie said.

"Me, too."

Wylie unzipped Amarina's shorts and pulled them off. Then she took her shoes off and finally her panties, which were wet from her orgasm.

When Amarina was laid bare for her, Wylie gently spread her legs and sat looking at the beauty that was Amarina.

"I can't get over how beautiful you are," she said. "God I've missed you."

She kissed her center, her clit, everything she could see. She sucked on her sweet, swollen lips and licked her slick clit. She was only exploring when Amarina cried out again.

"Baby, I'm just getting started," Wylie said.

"I can't help it. The things you make me feel…"

"Good. Well, you just relax and feel them."

Wylie licked around Amarina's opening. She dipped her tongue in and licked all around inside as deep as she could go. Amarina came again in no time.

Still not satisfied, Wylie sucked Amarina's clit between her lips while she ran her tongue over it and slipped her fingers inside. It took no time at all before Amarina cried out as she climaxed.

"I've had enough, babe. Now it's your turn."

Wylie couldn't argue. She was a throbbing wet mess and needed release. And she knew Amarina was the only one who could provide the kind of relief she required.

Amarina sat up.

"Now, stand up," she said.

Wylie stood, and Amarina unbuckled her belt, then unbuttoned and unzipped her shorts. She peeled them down her legs and slid them off over her boots.

"Dang, I've missed your body," Amarina said. "Now, take those boots off so I can have my way with you."

Wylie happily obliged. She didn't know how long she'd be able to hold out but was determined to make it last. She didn't want to come at Amarina's first touch but was terrified she would. She lay back on the bed and held her breath as Amarina climbed on top of her.

She dangled her breasts over Wylie, who took one with both hands and guided it to her mouth. She did the same thing with the other. She was dizzy with need.

Amarina rolled over to the side and bent to take one of Wylie's small breasts in her mouth. She sucked in the nipple and half the breast. Wylie gritted her teeth at the sensation, fighting off the orgasm she could feel building inside her.

As she continued to suck her nipple, Amarina moved her hand between Wylie's legs. She slid her fingers deep inside and used her thumb to rub her clit.

Wylie closed her eyes tight. She could see the lights starting to show behind her eyelids. She could feel the rush of energy coalescing in her center. It was no use. She couldn't fight it any longer. The energy burst apart and radiated throughout her body. She collapsed on the bed after the most powerful orgasm she'd ever had.

"We're so good together," she said as she took Amarina in her arms.

"We really are. And I'm glad that now we'll be together forever."

"Me, too, Amarina. Me, too."

About the Author

MJ Williamz was raised on California's central coast, which she left at age seventeen to pursue an education. She graduated from Chico State, and it was in Chico that she rediscovered her love of writing. It wasn't until she moved to Portland, however, that her writing really took off, with the publication of her first short story in 2003.

MJ is the author of ten books, including three Goldie Award winners. She has also had over thirty short stories published, most of them erotica, with a few romances and a few horrors thrown in for good measure. You can reach her at mjwilliamz@aol.com

Books Available from Bold Strokes Books

Amounting to Nothing by Karis Walsh. When mounted police officer Billie Mitchell steps in to save beautiful murder witness Merissa Karr, worlds collide on the rough city streets of Tacoma, Washington. (978-1-62639-728-6)

Becoming You by Michelle Grubb. Airlie Porter has a secret. A deep, dark, destructive secret that threatens to engulf her if she can't find the courage to face who she really is and who she really wants to be with. (978-1-62639-811-5)

Birthright by Missouri Vaun. When spies bring news that a swordswoman imprisoned in a neighboring kingdom bears the Royal mark, Princess Kathryn sets out to rescue Aiden, true heir to the Belstaff throne. (978-1-62639-485-8)

Crescent City Confidential by Aurora Rey. When romance and danger are in the air, writer Sam Torres learns the Big Easy is anything but. (978-1-62639-764-4)

Love Down Under by MJ Williamz. Wylie loves Amarina, but if Amarina isn't out, can their relationship last? (978-1-62639-726-2)

Privacy Glass by Missouri Vaun. Things heat up when Nash Wiley commandeers a limo and her best friend for a late drive out to the beach: Champagne on ice, seat belts optional, and privacy glass a must. (978-1-62639-705-7)

The Impasse by Franci McMahon. A horse packing excursion into the Montana Wilderness becomes an adventure of terrifying proportions for Miles and ten women on an outfitter led trip. (978-1-62639-781-1)

The Right Kind of Wrong by PJ Trebelhorn. Bartender Quinn Burke is happy with her life as a playgirl until she realizes she can't fight her feelings any longer for her best friend, bookstore owner Grace Everett. (978-1-62639-771-2)

Wishing on a Dream by Julie Cannon. Can two women change everything for the chance at love? (978-1-62639-762-0)

A Quiet Death by Cari Hunter. When the body of a young Pakistani girl is found out on the moors, the investigation leaves Detective Sanne Jensen facing an ordeal she may not survive. (978-1-62639-815-3)

Buried Heart by Laydin Michaels. When Drew Chambliss meets Cicely Jones, her buried past finds its way to the surface—will they survive its discovery or will their chance at love turn to dust? (978-1-62639-801-6)

Escape: Exodus Book Three by Gun Brooke. Aboard the Exodus ship *Pathfinder*, President Thea Tylio still holds Caya Lindemay, a clairvoyant changer, in protective custody, which has devastating consequences endangering their relationship and the entire Exodus mission. (978-1-62639-635-7)

Genuine Gold by Ann Aptaker. New York, 1952. Outlaw Cantor Gold is thrown back into her honky-tonk Coney Island past, where crime and passion simmer in a neon glare. (978-1-62639-730-9)

Into Thin Air by Jeannie Levig. When her girlfriend disappears, Hannah Lewis discovers her world isn't as orderly as she thought it was. (978-1-62639-722-4)

Night Voice by CF Frizzell. When talk show host Sable finally acknowledges her risqué radio relationship with a mysterious caller, she welcomes a *real* relationship with local tradeswoman Riley Burke. (978-1-62639-813-9)

Raging at the Stars by Lesley Davis. When the unbelievable theories start revealing themselves as truths, can you trust in the ones who have conspired against you from the start? (978-1-62639-720-0)

She Wolf by Sheri Lewis Wohl. When the hunter becomes the hunted, more than love might be lost. (978-1-62639-741-5)

Smothered and Covered by Missouri Vaun. The last person Nash Wiley expects to bump into over a two a.m. breakfast at Waffle House is her college crush, decked out in a curve-hugging law enforcement uniform. (978-1-62639-704-0)

The Butterfly Whisperer by Lisa Moreau. Reunited after ten years, can Jordan and Sophie heal the past and rediscover love or will differing desires keep them apart? (978-1-62639-791-0)

The Devil's Due by Ali Vali. Cain and Emma Casey are awaiting the birth of their third child, but as always in Cain's world, there are new and old enemies to face in post Katrina-ravaged New Orleans. (978-1-62639-591-6)

Widows of the Sun-Moon by Barbara Ann Wright. With immortality now out of their grasp, the gods of Calamity fight amongst themselves, egged on by the mad goddess they thought they'd left behind. (978-1-62639-777-4)

18 Months by Samantha Boyette. Alissa Reeves has only had two girlfriends and they've both gone missing. Now it's up to her to find out why. (978-1-62639-804-7)

Arrested Hearts by Holly Stratimore. A reckless cop with a secret death wish and a health nut who is afraid to die might be a perfect combination for love. (978-1-62639-809-2)

Capturing Jessica by Jane Hardee. Hyperrealist sculptor Michael tries desperately to conceal the love she holds for best friend, Jess, unaware Jess's feelings for her are changing. (978-1-62639-836-8)

Counting to Zero by AJ Quinn. NSA agent Emma Thorpe and computer hacker Paxton James must learn to trust each other as they work to stop a threat clock that's rapidly counting down to zero. (978-1-62639-783-5)

Courageous Love by KC Richardson. Two women fight a devastating disease, and their own demons, while trying to fall in love. (978-1-62639-797-2)

Pathogen by Jessica L. Webb. Can Dr. Kate Morrison navigate a deadly virus and the threat of bioterrorism, as well as her new relationship with Sergeant Andy Wyles and her own troubled past? (978-1-62639-833-7)

Rainbow Gap by Lee Lynch. Jaudon Vickers and Berry Garland, polar opposites, dream and love in this tale of lesbian lives set in Central Florida against the tapestry of societal change and the Vietnam War. (978-1-62639-799-6)

Steel and Promise by Alexa Black. Lady Nivrai's cruel desires and modified body make most of the galaxy fear her, but courtesan Cailyn Derys soon discovers the real monsters are the ones without the claws. (978-1-62639-805-4)

Swelter by D. Jackson Leigh. Teal Giovanni's mistake shines an unwanted spotlight on a small Texas ranch where August Reese is secluded until she can testify against a powerful drug kingpin. (978-1-62639-795-8)

Without Justice by Carsen Taite. Cade Kelly and Emily Sinclair must battle each other in the pursuit of justice, but can they fight their undeniable attraction outside the walls of the courtroom? (978-1-62639-560-2)

21 Questions by Mason Dixon. To find love, start by asking the right questions. (978-1-62639-724-8)

A Palette for Love by Charlotte Greene. When newly minted Ph.D. Chloé Devereaux returns to New Orleans, she doesn't expect her new job, and her powerful employer—Amelia Winters—to be so appealing. (978-1-62639-758-3)

By the Dark of Her Eyes by Cameron MacElvee. When Brenna Taylor inherits a decrepit property haunted by tormented ghosts, Alejandra Santana must not only restore Brenna's house and property but also save her soul. (978-1-62639-834-4)

Cash Braddock by Ashley Bartlett. Cash Braddock just wants to hang with her cat, fall in love, and deal drugs. What's the problem with that? (978-1-62639-706-4)